TWO BOOKS IN ONE

DETECTIVE ZACK

1 The Secret of Noah's Flood

2 The Mystery at Thunder Mountain

JERRY D. THOMAS

 **Pacific Press®**
Publishing Association

Nampa, Idaho | Oshawa, Ontario, Canada
www.pacificpress.com

Cover design by Gerald Lee Monks
Cover art and inside art by Kim Justinen

The author assumes full responsibility for the accuracy of all facts
and quotations as cited in this book.

The Secret of Noah's Flood originally published in 1992.
The Mystery at Thunder Mountain originally published in 1994.

Additional copies of this book can be obtained by calling toll-free
1-800-765-6955 or by visiting http://www.adventistbookcenter.com.

ISBN 978-0-8163-6129-8

September 2016

DETECTIVE ZACK

and The SECRET of Noah's Flood

Dedication

To my wife,
Kitty,
who is my inspiration,
and to my children:
Jonathan, Jennifer, and Jeremy.

Acknowledgment

The Geoscience Research Institute's field school
and materials provided many of the facts for
this book. And a special word of appreciation is
due to Dr. Ariel Roth and his staff, who took
time to review the manuscript.

Contents

CHAPTER ONE

Noah and the Tooth Fairy

**Daniel Boone National Forest
Twin Knobs Campground, Kentucky
June 27**

Why am I lying in my sleeping bag in a tent, writing in a notebook? What am I doing in Daniel Boone's forest? It's a long story, so I'll start at the beginning.

I'm trying to be still so I won't wake up my sister or brother, but it's not easy to write straight on this bumpy ground. Especially with a pencil in one hand and a flashlight in the other.

Anyway, it all started when my dad came home to tell us that we were going on a trip this summer. At first, I didn't want to go. I mean, I would miss out on summer camp and everything! But when he told me where we were going, I changed my mind. Because it's going to help me solve a mystery.

Really, I guess it started when my friend Bobby told me I was crazy. He wasn't being mean. He was just telling me what he thought. Friends are like that. And we're really good friends.

We have a fort in the woods behind my house. No one else knows where it is. One day, when we were building a secret lookout tower, I said something about Noah's ark.

"I wonder how this big rock got here?" Bobby had asked. He was standing on a rock that's bigger than my dad's van. It's the back wall of our fort, and our lookout station is on top.

"I'm sure the Flood left it there," I said as I carried another branch up to the top.

"What flood?"

"You know, the Flood. With Noah and the ark and everything?" I was sure he was teasing me.

"You're kidding me!"

I set the branch down and looked at him. "No, I'm not. How else do you think this rock got here?"

He laughed at me. "Nobody believes Noah and the Flood is a true story!"

"I do!"

"I guess you believe the Easter bunny and the tooth fairy are real too."

"What are you talking about? Don't you believe the stories in the Bible are real?" I thought he was just kidding. But he was being serious.

"Don't you know that scientists have proof that the world is millions of years old?"

"No, I never . . ."

"And they can prove that there never was a flood that covered the whole world."

I was getting confused. I knew that some scientists said those things, but I didn't think anyone believed them. "I don't think that's true. Who told you that?"

"We learned it in school. It's in my science book, so it has to be true."

"But the Bible says that Noah's flood really happened. How could the Bible be wrong?"

"My teacher says that the Bible is just an old storybook like Grimm's fairy tales or Mother Goose stories. She says that only some old-fashioned Christians still believe that stories like the Flood really happened. Are you an old-fashioned Christian?"

DETECTIVE ZACK

I didn't like being called old-fashioned. It sounded like old Mrs. Harper's dresses or a fire engine pulled by horses. But I didn't know what to say. I wanted to tell him to shut up, but that didn't seem right. Lucky for me, someone else spoke up.

"Zack, time for supper! Come home!" It was my mom.

"I gotta go," I mumbled and ran to my house.

I have to tell you, I was very confused. I thought everyone believed that the Bible was true, that the Flood was real. Right after Dad said the blessing, while he reached for the mashed potatoes, I threw the question at him.

"Dad, are the stories in the Bible true?"

Dad dropped the serving spoon into the gravy. My mom stopped pouring Kayla's juice and stared at me. Kayla's spoonful of corn stopped halfway to her mouth. (She's my sister and OK for a girl. But don't tell her I said so!) Even Alex stopped chewing for a minute (he's seven).

"What do you mean, Zack?" Dad fished out the spoon and used it to paint Kayla's potatoes with the brown gravy.

"I mean, are they real or just pretend—like fairy tales or Teenage Mutant Ninja Turtles?"

"Zack, we've always taught you that the Bible stories and people are real." Mom poured the juice as she talked. "Who told you they weren't?"

"Bobby told me that scientists can prove that the earth is millions of years old and that there never was a flood that covered the whole earth."

"And why do you think he might be right?" Dad asked.

"He said it was in his science book. And his teacher told him that the Bible was just an old storybook."

Dad looked across the salad bowl at me. Kayla was watching him too, waiting for his answer. Even Alex was listening.

"Part of what Bobby said is true."

"It is?" Kayla was shocked.

"Please let me finish." Dad looked sharply at her. "Bobby is right. Many scientists believe that the Bible is wrong, that there was no Flood. And most public schools don't teach that God created the earth and all the things that live on it. Instead, they teach evolution—the idea that over millions of years, the earth and the living things on it just kind of developed on their own."

"But can they prove it?" I asked.

"They think they can. But I think they're wrong."

"Can you prove that the Bible is right?"

"No. I can't prove it. That's why the Bible says we need faith. Zack, do you know what the Bible says faith is?"

"No."

This time Mom spoke up. "Zack, do you know what the word *evidence* means?"

"Isn't it like clues?"

"Yes. A detective looks for evidence or clues to solve a mystery. The Bible says that faith is the evidence of things not seen. What do you think that means?"

I chewed up a mouthful of mashed potatoes while I thought about that. "I guess it means that faith is believing something when there aren't enough clues to prove it."

"That's right, Zack."

"But if the whole world was covered with water, wouldn't there be some clues left behind? I wish I could tell Bobby some things that his scientists left out. Something that would show him that the Flood could have happened."

It was the next day when Dad came home with the good news about this summer.

But my flashlight batteries are running out! And I haven't even explained why I'm here or what I'm writing in my notebook. Well, I'll get to that tomorrow.

I'd better write myself a note to ask Dad for new batteries.

Interesting Things I've Seen

Important Words

Scientists: People who study all about science to find out how or when or why things happen (almost like detectives).

Faith: Believing in something even when there aren't enough clues to prove it.

Evidence: Clues about what really happened.

Detective: Someone who solves mysteries by searching for clues about what happened.

Evolution: The idea that the earth and the living things on it just kind of developed on their own over millions of years of time.

Noah's Flood Clues

Dad, I need batteries!

CHAPTER TWO

A Detective Takes the Case

**On the freeway
Driving through Kentucky
June 28**

You won't believe what I saw this morning! We were swimming in the lake at the campground, and I saw a big fish swimming right at the surface of the water! I called Kayla, and she saw it too. When it didn't disappear, we got closer. It swam away, but stayed at the top. We followed it around, and then some other kids joined us, and we tried to surround it and catch it. I grabbed it once, but it slipped away.

Near our campsite, I saw three deer eating grass. Their white tails went up like flags when they ran. We also saw one chipmunk, one woodchuck, and a lot of rabbits. Kayla and I picked some blackberries for lunch and skipped rocks on the lake.

Dad watched the rock-skipping for a minute; then he said, "See if you can hit that big green stump."

The stump was about as big as I am, but a lot more slimy! It was a long way out in the lake. Kayla couldn't throw that far, but I hit it—and when I did, it moved!

"Hey, Dad, look! The stump moved when I hit it."

He started throwing rocks too. And of course, he throws a lot harder than I do, so when he hit it, the stump really rocked.

"You're right, Zack. It's floating."

"Do stumps always float straight up like that, Dad?"

"I guess so. The roots are probably the heaviest part, so they stay down."

Anyway, after lunch, we packed up and drove off to find another campground. So now I'm riding in the van, and I'll try to write in my notebook again if the road isn't too bumpy.

But I still haven't explained why I'm writing in it. I didn't get to finish my story last night. Oh, yeah . . .

"Dad?"

"Yes, Zack."

"I need some more batteries for my flashlight."

"Your flashlight is already dead?"

"Well, first Alex used it on our way back from catching fireflies last night. And don't forget, I had it on when I was helping you find more wood for the fire."

"That's true, you were helping."

"Plus, I used it when Mom was looking for her sewing needle."

He looked over at Mom. "That's true," she said, "but we never did find it."

"And last night I had to use it to write in my notebook," I added.

"All right, all right," he laughed. "I think there are some new batteries in the camera case."

"Where's the camera case?"

"Well, I think it's right behind the seat, under the sleeping bags, right beside the cookstove. You can look for it when we stop at the next gas station."

DETECTIVE ZACK

By the time we pulled up to the pumps at a dusty gas station, I was ready . . . ready to jump out of the van and race to the restroom. And for once, I won and got there first. After that, of course, I had to see what kind of snacks and soda were for sale in the vending machines. Then Kayla ran up, tagged me, and shouted, "You're 'It'!"

Alex, Kayla, and I have been playing tag every time we stop. Kayla was "It" when we left after lunch, so she started this game. When Mom called us to the van, Alex was "It," so I'll have to watch out for him next time.

We were in the van and buckling our seat belts when I remembered the batteries. "Dad, wait a minute. I need to find those batteries."

Let me tell you something about our van. We were packed in like pickles in a pickle jar. It's not one of those big vans. It's just a minivan. With only one seat in the back, we had all the space behind it packed with food, clothes, and camping stuff. Usually, we argue about whose turn it is to sit by the door or by the window.

I looked at Alex and Kayla. They were already in their places and buckled up. Mom saw the argument coming. "Alex, Kayla, would you stand up for a minute so Zack can look for the camera case? Thanks, guys."

"Dad," I called out after a minute, "our tent's under the sleeping bags. I can't reach past it."

"Then you'll have to dig in from under the seat."

I looked at Mom. "Alex, Kayla," she said sweetly, "would you step out so Zack can look under the seat?"

They grumbled their way past me as I slid down to the floor in front. I pulled out a box of coloring books, a tape player, and my Micro Machines case. I thought I could see the camera case way in the back, so I stretched as far as I could and . . .

"Ouch! Mom!"

"What happened?"

"I think I found your needle."

I held up my right hand, with her needle sticking out of my finger. A little drop of blood was showing.

"Ow! I'm sorry." Her eyes were open wide, and she looked pale. Sometimes moms are like that.

"It's OK. It doesn't hurt that bad." I pulled out the needle and handed it to her. She held it away, like it was going to attack her next.

Anyway, I got the camera case and the batteries. Now, back to my notebook. I didn't get to finish last night, so I'll try to explain now. If I can keep from dripping blood on the pages.

Like I said, we had been talking about the Bible stories, especially Noah's flood. Did it really happen or not? I understood that there was no solid proof. It's not like someone was there to videotape it! But still, I wanted to know if there was some real evidence, some clues that it really happened.

That's when Dad came home with good news. He told us in the middle of pizza at supper one night. No, he wasn't in the middle of the pizza; we were just eating it when he told us. You know what I mean!

"How would you like to take a trip this summer?"

I thought of the trip we had taken the summer before. It was a nonstop drive to the school where Dad took summer classes. "Really, Dad, I'd like to stay home and go to summer camp with my friends and stuff like that."

"But we'll be going all the way to Utah."

"Where's Utah?" Alex wanted to know.

Dad got out the map of the United States. He traced a line with his finger all the way from our house in Maryland to Utah. "And look," he pointed out on the map, "we could stop in Texas and see your grandparents and cousins."

I liked that idea. But still, "Dad, why do you want to drive all the way to Utah?"

"I can go to a different kind of class there this summer. The teachers are scientists who will be showing us evidence that the Bible is correct when it talks about Noah's flood."

That sounded even better. "You mean these scientists will show us clues that the Bible story about the Flood really happened?"

"Yes."

"What are we waiting for? Let's go!"

"Whoa!" Dad laughed. "It'll take time to get ready. We're going to camp all along the way in national parks and forests. So we'll need our tents and sleeping bags, and our cookstove and lantern. But, Zack," he added, "there's something I must do first. Come up here to the head of the table."

I wasn't sure I wanted to leave my pizza. Alex was close enough to grab it. But I kept an eye on it while I walked around to Dad's chair. He opened a paper bag and pulled out a brown explorer's hat and a blue pin with big letters that said "DETECTIVE ZACK."

"Zack," he said, "I name you detective on this case. It's your job to solve the mystery of Noah's flood. Could it have happened? Is there any evidence?"

He put the hat on my head. Everyone clapped and cheered. "Yaaaay!"

Then he reached into the bag again and pulled out a blue notebook, the same color blue as the pin. "Zack, like all good detectives, you must keep a list of all the clues. Write down everything you see and hear that might be important. Keep this notebook with you everywhere we go."

I took the notebook. "Thank you, Dad," I said. "I accept the case." I took off my hat and bowed like a person in a play.

"Yaaaay!" Everyone cheered again.

"Now, Zack," Dad said as I got back to my pizza, "if you write down every clue we find, when we get back, you'll have something to teach Bobby about science. And about the Bible!"

"All right!"

So now you know why I've been writing in my notebook. I'm keeping a list of all the interesting things I see every day. And the important words I hear. You never know what will turn out to be a clue that supports the story of Noah's flood. And a good detective never misses a clue!

Interesting Things I've Seen

A chipmunk
Three deer
A very strange fish
A woodchuck
A floating stump

Important Words

Noah's Flood Clues

CHAPTER THREE

A Cave and a Candle

**Mammoth Cave National Park
Jellystone Park Campground, Kentucky
June 29**

I'd been to caves before, but never one like Mammoth Cave. It was great! After standing around in the hot sun waiting for our tour to start, stepping into the cave felt good—like going into an air-conditioned store. I took off my detective hat to cool my head. The tour guide began explaining cave stuff right away.

"The strange rock formations [for-may-shuns] you will see are called stalactites [stah-lak-tights] and stalagmites [stah-lag-mights]. The ones hanging from the ceiling like icicles are stalactites. The ones growing up from the floor are stalagmites. Mammoth Cave is a living cave. That means that the stalactites and stalagmites are still growing. They are still being formed today, just like they have been for millions of years."

I looked at Dad. "Millions of years? We won't learn anything about Noah's flood here."

Dad turned toward me and winked. "Let's just listen and watch while we're here. Maybe we can find some hidden clues."

The tour guide was pointing to a stalactite that was almost touching a stalagmite. "Watch for the drip of water." We watched, and one drop fell. "As the drop of water passes over the formations, it leaves behind a tiny bit of the minerals it carries. Slowly those minerals build up on the surfaces. So, with every drop, the stalagmite grows a little taller and the stalactite grows a little longer. At the rate this water is dripping, we believe that these two will grow together in about ten thousand years."

Alex spoke loud enough for everyone to hear. "Is that a long time, Mom?"

The people on the tour all laughed. I was embarrassed. Little brothers are like that sometimes. "Let's not wait around to see," the tour guide said as she led the way farther down into the cave.

Soon we were in a big room. And when I say big, I mean big! It was big enough to put a whole football stadium in, including the seats and the lights!

The tour guide pointed to the tiny stream of water running along the bottom of the room. "It's hard to believe that a room this big could have been carved out of solid rock by a little stream like that, but it was. Over millions of years, that stream washed away this much rock!" She waved her arm around the room.

I'll say it's hard to believe, I thought.

"Now I want to give you an idea how this cave must have looked to the first explorers who came in." She moved over to a metal box. "In a minute, I'm going to turn out all the lights. It will be totally dark."

"Oooooh," everyone said.

"Then I'll light one candle to show you how much light the early cave explorers had. Children, don't leave your parents alone in the dark. They might get scared, and I don't want any crying parents to take care of."

Kayla grabbed my arm and stood close to me. I guess she was scared or something. Sisters are like that sometimes. I looked around and saw that Dad was standing next to Mom, holding Alex. We scooted over next to them. Just so they wouldn't worry.

"Everyone ready? Here we go!" The lights went out, and it was dark. I mean really dark. I couldn't tell if my eyes were open or closed! I couldn't see anything at all. I waved my hands in front of my face to see if I could see them.

"Ouch!"

"Sorry, Kayla."

Then the tour guide lighted the candle. The yellow light made giant shadows on the walls and ceiling.

"Oooooh," everyone said again.

The candlelight seemed a lot brighter than I thought it would.

"Now watch this." She used the candle to light a short torch. "Early explorers used torches to explore the dark passages. When they wanted to see how big a room like this was, they would do this." She swung her arm and threw the torch up to a ledge high above the floor.

"Oooooh," we all said.

The torch flickered brightly, and I tried to imagine exploring a cave like this. I bet Bobby and I could have done it.

"Mom, are there any caves near our house?"

"I hope not!" she exclaimed.

I wonder why she said that?

Later, back at the campground, we had a lot of fun too. There was a pool and a waterslide. We swam until it was nearly dark; then we changed and came back to the camp outdoor theater and watched Yogi Bear cartoons for a while. Then somebody put on a Yogi Bear costume and went around shaking hands with the little kids. The Yogi in the costume didn't look "smarter than your average bear," but I guess Alex liked him. Little brothers are like that.

It was dark by the time we started making supper. Dad lighted the lantern and set it on the picnic table so we could see. It was my turn to help Mom make supper. Dad, Kayla, and Alex started setting up the beds in the tents.

"Zack, the cookstove needs to be pumped up before we light it."

"No problem, Mom." I popped out the little handle and started pumping. It was harder than I thought. ". . . forty-eight, forty-nine, fifty. It's ready, Mom," I panted.

"Thanks. Now if you'll open the beans, I'll chop

the lettuce and tomatoes. And open a can of olives too."

I started twisting the stubborn can opener around the tops of the cans. "Mom," I asked, "what kind of candle do you think that was in the cave today? You remember, the one that guide lighted after the lights were out? I think it was brighter than this lantern!"

"It was a normal candle, Zack. It just seemed brighter because your eyes had adjusted to the darkness."

"What?"

"You know that the pupils in your eyes, the black part, get larger when it's dark."

"Yes."

"Well, the cave was so dark that your pupils got as large as they could. So when the candle was lighted, it seemed much brighter than usual."

"So if that candle were out here now, it wouldn't seem bright at all."

"No, not next to this lantern or the campfire. And maybe there's a good lesson in this, Zack. A lesson about truth."

I looked at Mom and shook my head. "I don't understand."

"People who don't know much about God and the beginning of this world might think that the scientists' stories of millions of years and no Flood are pretty bright ideas. But when you compare those ideas to the truth from the Bible, they seem pale and weak."

I looked at her eyes shining in the firelight. "Thanks, Mom, I like that. I want the real truth, not somebody's weak ideas. I'm glad we're going on this trip. I didn't get to ask Dad if he saw any hidden clues in the cave yet."

"I'm sure you'll have time tomorrow," she said. "We have to leave early and drive all day."

While I was giving her a hug, I saw something.

"Hey, look! A bat!"

"What! Where?"

"It just swooped over the fire. Look, there it is again!"

Mom dived toward the tent, nearly knocking me down. "Keep it away from me!" she screamed.

"Aw, Mom. It's already gone. Come on, let's eat." I don't know what she was so upset about. It looked cute to me. I guess moms are just like that.

Interesting Things I've Seen

A big cave room
A totally *dark*, big cave room
A bright candle
A flying torch
A flying bat
Stalactites
Stalagmites

Important Words

Formations: Rocks in layers or shapes—sometimes weird shapes.

Stalactites: Rock formations hanging from the ceiling of a cave. They look like dirty icicles.

Stalagmites: Rock formations growing up from the floor of a cave. Many look like dirty, upside-down ice-cream cones.

Living cave: A cave in which the stalactites and stalagmites are still growing.

Minerals: The stuff in water that forms stalactites and stalagmites.

Noah's Flood Clues

CHAPTER FOUR

Tomato Plants and Muddy Feet

Ouachita National Forest
Flatside Wilderness Campground, Arkansas
July 1

I didn't get to write anything in the notebook last night. We had trouble finding the camping place, and by the time we stopped for the night, it was completely dark. That made it extra hard to set up the tents and make supper.

We just kept following a dirt road into the Ozark Mountains, and we ended up in the middle of nowhere. I mean, there was nothing and nobody for miles. We finally stopped at a large clearing on the side of a mountain. You'd have thought the place would be quieter than a schoolroom in summer. But when I got out of the car, so much noise blasted my eardrums that I couldn't hear myself think. It sounded like a chainsaw party at an airport!

"Where's all this noise coming from?" I shouted at Dad.

"It must be crickets and other insects! It was quieter in the car, with the engine running!"

We rushed around to set up the tents, and when we were finished, Kayla and I had a plan.

"Dad, let's take a flashlight and go see what's making all the noise," we shouted.

"OK. Let me set up the cookstove for your mother." He was ready in a few minutes, and we stalked off toward the nearest trees. When we got to the first tree, we shined the light at it. But the creature or creatures in it that were making the noise stopped—though you could barely tell because of the noise from the other trees.

"What is it? Do you see anything?" We searched through the tree but saw nothing except leaves. At the next tree, the same thing happened. We looked all through the branches and even on the

ground under the tree, but we couldn't find anything.

"This time, let's sneak up on it," I shouted. So we
turned off the flashlight and walked in the dark to
the next tree. Then I snapped on the light, and we
saw one of the noisemakers! It was a green tree
frog, sitting on the edge of a green leaf, peeping at
the top of its lungs. It wasn't any bigger than a
quarter. There must have been thousands of frogs
in those trees, all singing like crazy.

We shouted the story to Mom, and she was
amazed too. Anyway, since we couldn't talk or
anything, we went straight to bed after eating.
When the sun woke me up in the morning, it was
quiet. I looked for the tree frogs, but I couldn't find
even one.

Yesterday, right after we crossed the Missis-
sippi River, I remembered to ask Dad about the
cave. I put on my detective cap and started asking
questions.

"OK, Dad. How do we explain the millions of
years it took to carve out a cave that big?"

"That's a good question, Zack. Let's start by
thinking about how caves are formed. Usually,
caves are found where the rocks underground are
a kind of rock called limestone. Limestone dissolves slowly in water."

"What do you mean?" I asked. "Does it get soft and fall apart like mud?"

"Not exactly. It's more like a lollipop. It just gets smaller and smaller until it's gone. Anyway, as water seeps through the limestone . . ."

"What do you mean, seeps?"

"The water flows through and around the limestone. It's like my tomato plant on the back porch. You turn on the water hose and let some water trickle into the big pot, and pretty soon, the water is flowing out onto the ground from the holes in the bottom."

I remembered. "So that water seeps through from the top to the bottom."

"Right," Dad said. "Caves are being formed today the same way. When it rains, water seeps through the limestone and forms underground streams or rivers like you saw yesterday. And as the water slowly dissolves the limestone rock, the space inside—the cave—gets bigger."

"So that cave we were in is still growing," I said.

"Yes. So scientists have looked at how much it grows in one year and have decided that to get as big as it is, it must have been growing for millions of years," Dad explained.

"So, are they right?"

"Let me answer that like this. Do you remember

the tomato plants I raised on the back porch last summer?"

Uh-oh! I was afraid I knew where this story was going. "Yes."

"And do you remember the day I asked you to water them for me?"

I was right. That was not a good day. "Yes," I answered. "I turned the water on more than just a trickle and left it on too long."

"And?"

"And it blasted one tomato plant right out of the pot!"

Dad laughed. "Well, not really. But the water seeped through the dirt in the pot so fast and for so long that it washed all the dirt right out from around the plant's roots. And when enough dirt was washed out the bottom, the plant fell over."

I groaned. "I remember the mud that ran all over the porch floor."

"Now think about the cave again. If the same amount of water was seeping through every year, it would grow at the same speed every year. But what if a lot of water had to seep through? What if . . ."

"What if there was a flood!" I said quickly. "It would wash out the limestone much faster than it is washing out today."

"Right. If the flood covered the whole earth, then when it went down after the rain stopped, that water had to go somewhere. It would be flowing down through big rivers and seeping quickly into rocks like limestone and carving out big caves in a short time."

"So caves are a pretty good clue that there was a flood," I agreed. "It makes a lot more sense that a flood of water washed out those rocks instead of just a drip. That makes the millions of years seem like a pretty pale idea!" I looked at my mom, and she smiled. "But wait a minute. What about the stalactites and stalagmites? The tour guide said they took millions of years to grow."

Dad had to think about it for a minute. "OK. What do we do when the dog wants to come into the house, and his feet are muddy?"

Murphy, our dog, has hairy feet, and he always finds mud even when it's not raining. "We put him in the bathtub and wash his feet off."

"And the bathtub is coated with mud."

"I know. I have to rinse it out," I groaned.

"What would happen if we never rinsed it out? What if the water always ran out, but not the mud?"

"The mud would get thicker and thicker on the bottom of the tub."

"Right. Now, if you washed the dog's feet every day, how long would it be until the tub was full of mud?"

That didn't make sense at first. "How would I know?"

"Think about it."

"Well, it depends on how dirty his feet are."

"That's right. The dirtier his feet are, the faster the tub would fill with mud. Now, stalactites are formed as the minerals in the water stick while the water drips off. So what do Murphy's dirty feet have to do with stalactites?"

"The dirtier the water is—I mean, the more minerals and stuff in it—the quicker the stalactites would grow," I figured out.

"And what do you think the floodwater would look like? All clean and pure?"

"No! It would be muddy and full of minerals and junk. Just right for growing stalactites. So stalactites and stalagmites are good clues that there was a flood too."

"Right you are, son. And of course, those stalactites and stalagmites have been growing since the Flood too."

"Thanks, Dad, for helping me understand. And . . . Dad?"

"Yes?"

DETECTIVE ZACK

"Sorry about your tomato plant last year."
"That's OK. I already forgot about it."
I guess dads are just like that.

Interesting Things I've Seen

Thousands of green tree frogs (But I only saw one.)

Important Words

Limestone: A kind of rock that can be dissolved by water.

Noah's Flood Clues

Caves: Large caves could have been washed out of the soft limestone faster if a lot of water was seeping through, like it would be if there was a flood.

Stalactites and stalagmites: Dirty floodwater, full of minerals, could have helped them grow faster than they are growing today.

CHAPTER FIVE

Wind, Rocks, and Dinosaur Walks

Clayton Lake State Park
Clayton, New Mexico
July 10

I haven't written in my notebook for a long time. I haven't really looked for any clues since our stop in Texas to see my grandparents and all my cousins. But I did see some very interesting things that I need to write down. And I will, if I can keep the wind from blowing my notebook away!

DETECTIVE ZACK

This campsite is neat. We set our tents up right next to the lake. But the really interesting things are the rocks. All around us stand big rocks that have weird, round shapes. One is as tall as a basketball goal, but it's shaped like a loaf of bread. Some are as big as cars or houses.

Walking between these big rocks is like walking down the streets of a big city and looking up at round skyscrapers and buildings. Except the rocks aren't *that* tall. And they're a lot of fun to climb!

Kayla, Alex, and I climbed to the top of one big rock that was shaped like a giant mushroom. We waved at Mom and Dad back at the campsite. "Hey, Dad!" I yelled. "What shaped all these rocks like this?"

"I can't hear you!" he yelled back. So when we finished climbing and went to eat, I asked him again.

Instead of answering, he asked me a question. "What do you think the tour guide at the cave would say?"

"I don't know, but probably that it took millions of years."

He laughed. "You're right. Scientists might tell you that at one time, this area was all level ground."

Alex was listening. He asked, "Did the rocks all grow here?"

"No," Dad said. "When the ground here was level, it was level with the tops of those rocks. Where we are sitting would have been twenty feet under the ground."

I looked out over the lake. "So the lake wasn't here then either."

"Not like it is now, anyway. Some of the rocks here were hard and some soft. Many scientists will tell you that over millions of years, the softer rocks were worn away by the rain and the wind. Now only the harder rocks are left. When the wind and rain wear away rocks and soil, it's called erosion [e-row-shun]."

"So that's why the rocks are in such weird shapes," I said. "When the soft parts washed away, the hard parts were just left hanging around. But I'd say the Flood washed the soft rocks away, not millions of years."

"I think you're right," Dad agreed. "The Bible says that when the rain stopped, God sent a great wind to dry up the earth. I think that wind and the floodwaters washed out the soft rocks and left this like we see it today."

So here I am, with a strong wind trying to blow the pages right out of my notebook. Now, back to the things I saw in Texas.

On that first night, we went to my grandma's house. She took us to an amusement park, Six Flags Over Texas, with all our aunts and uncles and cousins. The rides were neat! But I stayed off the roller coasters. I knew they would make me throw up!

Then, that weekend, we went to a place where you can see dinosaur tracks in the rocks. The tracks run right down the middle of a dry creek bed. We hiked out there and tried to follow in the footsteps.

"Hey, Mom, look at me!" Alex called out. He was standing with both feet in one dinosaur footprint! I could put both of my feet in one too. We tried to step from one footprint to the next, but they were too far apart.

"And this was not even a very big dinosaur," Dad laughed.

"Were there really big dinosaurs, Dad?" Alex asked.

"I think so, Alex. Scientists have found very big bones that belonged to some large beasts."

"I know," I added. "I've seen their skeletons in a museum."

"I have too," Dad said. "But usually when dinosaur bones or fossils are found, there are only a few pieces lying around together. The scientists have found only a few whole skeletons, so sometimes they guess what the whole skeleton would look like. And then they guess what the dinosaur would look like if it were alive."

"So there was no such thing as a tyrannosaur or a stegosaurus?"

"Probably there was. But with some of the other kinds, we don't know for sure. Sometimes it's almost as hard as looking at a pile of Legos and guessing what kind of truck you could make."

I thought of another question. "Dad, don't scientists say that dinosaurs lived millions of years before there were any people?"

"Yes. That's what some of them say."

Alex spoke up. "Daddy, what does the Bible say about dinosaurs?"

"The Bible doesn't say anything about dinosaurs, Alex."

"So doesn't that mean that there never really were any dinosaurs?"

"No. Dinosaurs could have lived on the earth before the Flood. They could have lived after the Flood, but not in the place where the people in the Bible lived. Or maybe they died during the Flood."

"I guess there wasn't any room for them on the ark!" Alex said.

Dad laughed. "Not all dinosaurs were giant creatures. Many dinosaurs were no bigger than your dog, Murphy."

I guessed, "Maybe they just didn't come when Noah called!"

The other fun stuff we did was fireworks on the Fourth of July at the house of my other grandparents. At Papa and Mema's (that's what we call them), we set off firecrackers and skyrockets. Lots of our cousins were there too.

We took a trip to the beach the next week. I was exploring the beach while Dad and Papa went fishing on a pier. I searched through tons of seashells and found a whole sand dollar. When I ran down the pier to show Dad, he and Papa were walking back toward me.

"Look what I found!" I shouted. While they were looking at it, I asked, "Did you catch anything?"

Dad was just saying, "No, we haven't even had a bite," when we heard someone far down the pier shouting.

"Hey, one of your fishing poles just went over the side!"

We ran as fast as we could to the place where they had left their poles. Sure enough, one of them was gone. And the other one was bending toward the water. Dad grabbed it quickly and started pulling back on the line.

"Whatever it is, it's big!" he said.

"It could be a shark," Papa said. "I've seen some big ones pulled in here."

"A shark!" I shouted. "Pull it in, Dad. I want to see it!"

"I'm trying," he grunted as he strained on the pole. Slowly it lifted, until suddenly, right on top of the water, we could see what he'd caught. But it wasn't a shark. It was a stingray!

"Wow!" I said. The ray was wider than I am tall. "Hold it there, Dad." But the stingray was tired of bothering with us. With a flip of his fins, he was gone. The fishing line snapped like a thread.

"I've never seen one like that," Papa said. "It was worth losing a fishing pole to see it."

But when Dad reeled in his broken line, Papa's pole came in too. The stingray had tangled them up together.

Pretty cool, don't you think?!

Interesting Things I've Seen

Rocks shaped like big loaves of bread and giant mushrooms

Millions of seashells

A sand dollar—a sea creature skeleton that looks like a silver dollar coin

A stingray

Important Words

Erosion: The wearing away of rocks and soil by wind and rain.

Noah's Flood Clues

Weird-shaped rocks: They could have been formed when the floodwaters went down and God sent wind to dry the land.

CHAPTER SIX

The Top of the World Is Wet

Pike National Forest
Top of the World Campground, Colorado
July 11

If I can keep from dripping on the pages, I'll try to write down what has happened since yesterday. I sure learned one thing, though—it's cold in the mountains, especially when you're wet.

Our first stop yesterday was at a place called the Garden of the Gods. It's a big park filled with gigantic slabs of rock. The ranger at the visitor center said that they were made of red and white sandstone. Anyway, these slabs, mostly great big, flat rocks standing on end, were in weird shapes.

We found that many of these strange shapes had names. "What do they call that one, Dad?" I asked. It looked like four shark fins sticking out of a big whale's back.

"I believe that it's called 'Kissing Camels.' "

"Kissing Camels?" I said. "That's a dumb name. Probably named by some girl." Kayla hit me.

We drove around the park, and Mom pointed out the other famous rocks. "And that one is called 'Cathedral Spires.' I guess someone thought it looked like church steeples."

"Look out, Dad!" Alex yelled.

Dad swerved from one side of the road to the other. "What is it? Look out for what?"

"Up there! That rock is going to fall on the road." Alex pointed to a big, round rock, way up on the edge of a cliff.

"Alex, that rock is called 'Balanced Rock.' It's been sitting there for years without falling. It just looks like it will fall any minute," Mom explained.

From the park, we could see Pike's Peak, the highest mountain in that area. It was a good thing we looked at it when we did. The peak was soon covered with clouds. In fact, dark clouds were slowly filling the sky. After lunch, we drove up into the mountains to find a camping spot.

When we pulled up to the campsite, we could hear thunder rumbling. "Zack, we'd better set up those tents in a hurry," Dad said.

He and I jumped out and quickly went to work. Just about the time we got everything out of the car, the rain started. "Where do we set the tents up now?" I shouted.

"As long as it's not in a hole, it doesn't really matter. Every place will be wet soon." Dad grabbed the hammer and the stakes. "Put the sleeping bags and other stuff back in the van until the tents are ready."

To make a wet story short, we ate supper standing up under the back hatch of the van and then crawled into our damp tents. The rain kept falling, and it sounded like we were on the inside of a drum. "Daddy," Alex called out, "come in and tell us a story."

Mom and Dad both crawled into our tent. Alex sat in Mom's lap, and Dad crawled in between Kayla and me. Lightning flashed around us, and the mountain rumbled with thunder.

"Daddy, will the lightning strike us here?" Kayla was worried.

"I think we'll be safe, honey. Don't worry."

I tried to help. "Kayla, there's no way lightning could strike us here."

"Why?"

"We're up in the clouds, and the lightning is striking down at the ground." That sounded good until a flash of lightning as bright as day shook the mountain under us. The rain kept drumming on the tent roof. We all huddled closer together.

Dad spoke up. "Do you think Noah and his family felt like this that first night the ark floated in the Flood? They must have been scared too."

Mom added, "And the whole world outside the ark's door was being destroyed. Their home and everything were gone. All they had left was their faith in God's promise to save them."

"I know what they felt good about," Alex spoke up. "They had lots of animals to play with."

"Ha," I laughed, "and lots of animals to clean up after!"

"And what about breakfast?" asked Mom. "How would you like a hungry elephant trumpeting you awake?"

"Or a lion roaring? Or an eagle screaming?" Kayla added. Alex just smiled and nodded. Little brothers are like that.

"Zack," Dad said, "there is some evidence for Noah's flood that we can't see on a trip like this.

But it's important, so you might want to write it in the notebook."

Luckily, my notebook was in my pillowcase. I had left my hat in the car so it would stay dry. "OK, tell me."

"All right. The Bible isn't the only book that tells about a worldwide flood. There are flood stories from nearly every old civilization [civi-li-za-shun]."

"What's a civilization?" Kayla asked.

"It's a group of people who live together and form their own way of life. The children of Israel in the Bible were one of the old civilizations. In every part of the world, people had their own ways and their own stories. But most of them tell about a flood that covered the earth and destroyed everything."

"Are all the flood stories like the one in the Bible?" I asked.

"No. They are all different. There are different heroes and different reasons why the flood came. Remember, none of the other old civilizations worshiped the true God."

"Why is that good evidence for Noah's flood?" asked Kayla.

"Kayla, what if you ran into the visitor center at Garden of the Gods and told the rangers that you saw two real camels kissing outside?"

She laughed. "No one would believe me."

"But what if all of us said we saw them too?"

She thought. "Well, I'm sure some people would believe us. But some would think we were all crazy."

"OK, but what if ten or twenty other people came in and said they saw kissing camels too? Don't you think the rangers would believe it then?" She nodded, and he went on. "The same is true for the flood stories. When so many people tell of a flood that covered the earth, so many people who don't even know each other, it makes it seem likely that a big flood really happened."

I spoke up. "Did all the stories come from the people who lived near the Israelites? Could it have been just a really bad flood in that area?"

"Seven flood stories come from the Middle East area. But three come from Africa, and six come from South America. And the North American Indians told thirteen different stories of a flood."

"Wow! You almost have to believe that something big happened all over the world."

"That's right," Dad said. "Now listen. The rain has stopped, and maybe the storm is over. Everyone go to sleep, and we'll probably wake up to beautiful, blue skies."

Interesting Things I've Seen

"Kissing Camels"
A balanced rock (It looked like it was about to fall.)
More strange rock shapes

Important Words

Sandstone: Rock made up of sand cemented together.
Civilization: A group of people who live together and form their own way of life.

Noah's Flood Clues

Flood stories: Stories of a worldwide flood were told in old civilizations all over the world—so something probably happened to the whole world.

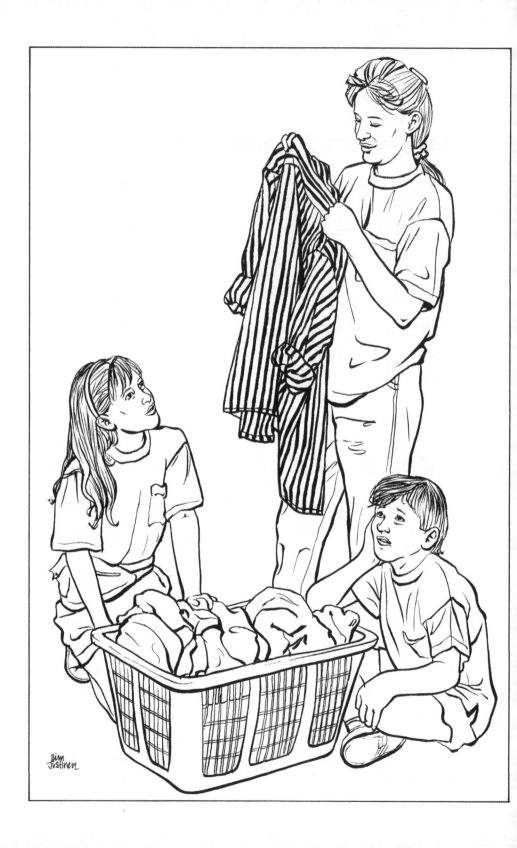

CHAPTER SEVEN

Mountains and Waterfalls

Colorado National Monument
Saddlehorn Campground, Colorado
July 12

It was a great summer day at camp. I was just floating away on my tube in the lake, dipping my hands and feet into the water, splashing a little on my face. But wow, this water was cold. Too cold. And why was I so cold, there in the sunshine? What in the world, I thought . . . and zap, just like that, I was awake. But I was still floating in water. Well, almost. My pillow was soaked, and my sleeping bag was wet down to my knees.

I rolled over and looked up just in time to catch a big cold drop right in the eye. The tent was leaking right at the top of the door zipper. "Oh, yuck," I said out loud.

"Zack, is that you? Come on out and help me build a fire." Dad was already carrying wet wood up to the campfire pit. I got my damp coat on and went out to help. The sky rumbled and flashed, and the fire wouldn't start no matter what we did.

Soon other voices were calling out from the tents. "Hey, it's wet in here." "Is the fire going yet?" "What's for breakfast?" And just as they stepped out into the morning cold, the rain started again.

Everyone dashed for the van. The doors slammed, the engine roared, and we sat shivering as we waited for the heat to come on. "You know, Zack, we might as well go out and pack up the tents now, since we're wet anyway," Dad said.

I guess he was right. It was a good plan. Until the hail started falling. Bonk, a hail stone bounced off my head. Mom opened her window and shouted, "Just wad it all up and throw it in. We'll drive to a laundromat and dry it all there."

So we did it as quickly as we could and were

soon inching our way back down the mountain toward the big city of Denver and the nearest clothes dryers.

After a quick change of clothes and breakfast at a McDonald's, we found a laundromat and filled every dryer. Dad and I were out in the parking lot, folding up the wet tents. He said, "We must look pretty strange to people driving by."

"I don't care," I said. "I'd rather look strange than feel wet and cold."

Later, after everything was dry and clean, we had lunch at Casa Bonita. That place is wild! We ate our food next to the waterfall. Yes, there really is a waterfall, right in the restaurant. And every few minutes, a diver would step out beside the falls and dive into the pool at the bottom. Also, there were arcade games, puppet shows for little kids, and "Black Bart's Cave," where you had to fight your way past pirates and giant spiders to find the treasure (not really, but it was fun to pretend).

Soon we were headed west again, toward Utah. I was staring at the mountains as we climbed higher and higher. But something seemed wrong. "Dad, why is everyone passing us?"

"The van has a problem. You remember how it was losing power yesterday? Well, it's worse now.

The higher we go in the mountains, the less power the engine has."

"Why? Is it just harder to pull all of our stuff?"

"No, it has to do with oxygen [ox-e-jen]. Car engines breathe in oxygen just like we do. The higher you go, the less air there is—so the less oxygen. You'll find that out when we get to Utah and you start to run and play. You'll get tired and out of breath quickly."

"Will we be staying on a mountain in Utah?"

"Yes, right at the top. Anyway, when the van doesn't get enough oxygen, it can't burn the gas very well, so it doesn't have much power."

All this time, we were going slower and slower. "Is our van going to make it over the mountains?" I asked.

"We'll know soon. This is the highest part right ahead of us. If we can get to the top, I'm sure we'll make it to Utah." Dad turned on the blinkers and stayed close to the right side of the road so others could go by.

I wasn't sure we would make it, but slowly we climbed to the top—and picked up speed going down the other side. Soon we were looking for the turnoff to our campsite.

"We're not really going up there, are we?" Mom was pointing up at the cliffs toward which we were headed. When we began climbing up the side of the cliff on a small, curvy road, I could tell by the look on her face that she wasn't very happy.

The campground was right up on the clifftop, called a plateau (plah-tow). It was a wide area, as flat as a table, with nothing but rocks and short bushes. After the tents were set up, I wanted to go exploring, but Mom insisted that we all stay together.

We walked together toward the edge of the cliff, where a ranger was pointing out something to some other campers. "These monoliths [monn-o-liths]—these tall, skinny fingers of stone—were formed by millions of years of the wind and rain's erosion." I looked out at one of the big rock statues. It looked about as big as a tennis court on top, and the sides went almost straight down. "That big one there," the ranger said, pointing to an enormous rock standing out by itself, "is called Independence [in-d-pen-dents] Rock. It is 500 feet tall."

"Ooooooh," everyone said.

"Once this whole area was level with us here. But now, all that is left is this plateau and these majestic rocks. Isn't it amazing what millions of years of erosion can do?" The ranger laughed as he walked away.

"Either millions of years or lots of water!" Dad said, and he winked at me. We walked on and saw "Window Rock," a rock monolith with a hole right through it. There was also one called the "Devil's Kitchen." It was probably named by a mother who was tired of cooking on camping trips.

"Look at that!" Alex said, pointing to the edge of the cliff. "A squirrel just ran off the edge." But the squirrel popped back up as he said it. While we watched, several more rock squirrels ran along and over the edge and back up. "See, Mom," Alex said, "the squirrels aren't afraid." Mom just shuddered and grabbed his hand.

At the evening program, the ranger told more about the history of the area and its first explorers. Later, we walked back to our tents in the dark. Well, it wasn't really dark, because the full moon was shining out of a clear sky. No clouds were in sight, I was happy to notice.

"Stay close together," Mom said. "I don't want anyone falling over the edge."

Of course, we were probably a thousand feet from the edge, but it was nice to know that she cared. Moms are just like that, I guess.

Suddenly, something "whooshed" past us in the air. "What was that?" cried Kayla.

"A bat!" Mom yelled. "Run!"

Now I was afraid that *she* was going to jump over the edge. "Just be still," Dad said. "Listen. It's not a bat. Hear the wind in its wings? It's a nighthawk."

Then we saw it clearly in the moonlight. And it was a nighthawk, out eating mosquitoes and other bugs. In fact, we saw seven more before we got back to the tents.

"Well, it could have been a bat," Mom said, watching the sky carefully. After our worship and prayer, we got into our sleeping bags. She zipped them all the way up. "No sleepwalking tonight, you guys," she said.

"Aw, Mom, go to bed," I said. Poor Mom. With "bats" and "cliffs" all around her, I wonder if she slept at all.

Interesting Things I've Seen

Waterfall divers
"Black Bart's cave"
Seven rock squirrels
Eight nighthawks

Important Words

Oxygen: What we must breathe to stay alive. Cars need it too.
Plateau: Flat land on a mountain.
Monoliths: Very tall rocks.

Noah's Flood Clues

CHAPTER EIGHT

Clues From a Dinosaur's Lunch

Brian Head Ski Resort
Brian Head, Utah
July 13

"Utah at last!" Dad said as we crossed the state border this morning.

"How much farther to the place we're going?" I asked. We'd never really talked about where in Utah Dad's classes were being taught.

"It's still about six hours to Brian Head. It's way down in the southwest corner of the state."

"Brian who?" asked Alex.

"Not Brian who, Alex, Brian Head," I tried to explain. "It's just the name of the place, not a person."

"I wish we had time to go by Dinosaur National Monument. It's not too far from here," Dad said.

"Do they have real dinosaurs there?" Alex asked.

"No. It's really a dinosaur graveyard. More dinosaur bone fossils have been found there than any other place on earth."

"I never thought of dinosaurs living here in America," I said. "Did they find any whole skeletons or just pieces?"

"I believe that fifteen whole skeletons have been found, and parts of many others. And there are still more being dug up every year. If you could go there, you could watch the paleontologists [pay-lee-un-tall-uh-jists] working to remove the fossils from the ground. Paleontologists are scientists who study bones and fossils."

"Are you sure we don't have time to go there?" Kayla asked.

"Sorry, but my classes start tomorrow. We need to get to Brian Head this afternoon."

I was curious about that dinosaur graveyard. "Dad, how did all those dinosaur bones get to that one spot?"

"That's a good question, Zack. First of all, scientists think that many of the dinosaurs of earth died suddenly. They aren't sure why. But they believe that there was a large river flowing through what is now the graveyard. For whatever reasons, when the dinosaurs in this area died, many of their bodies fell into the river and floated downstream to the point where the bones are found today. At that place, the river became clogged up, and the dinosaur bodies were eaten or sank."

"It would take a pretty big river to float dinosaurs, wouldn't it?"

Dad laughed. "Yes, it would. Anyway, the scientists think that after a long time, the sand and mud where the dinosaurs sank became rock. And the dinosaur bones became fossils when the sand or mud turned into rock, because the skeleton turned to stone also."

I thought about that. It was time for a little detective work. "Now wait a minute. The dinosaurs died suddenly; then their giant bodies floated away to be covered with sand and mud that turned into rock. Doesn't that sound like Noah's flood to you?"

"It does to me," Dad agreed. "The story of the flood fits the scientific facts of the case. Some paleontologists may have other ideas about what happened, but the Bible's flood story makes the most sense to me."

"It would take a flood just to float those big, fat dinosaur bodies away and pile them up," Alex added.

"And I'll give you another clue," Dad said. "If those dinosaurs lived near this area before they died, what do you think they ate?"

I could only guess. "Probably either each other or some kind of plants."

"The dinosaurs they found were ones that ate plants. But though they have found lots of dinosaur fossils, they have found very few plant fossils—and nothing much that could have fed dinosaurs' huge appetites. What does that tell you?"

"Well, it must mean that those dinosaurs didn't live near here. They must have lived somewhere else," I decided.

"There is little fossil evidence of dinosaur food anywhere in those rocks. So they must have lived a long way from where they were found," Dad said.

"That makes sense if you believe in a flood that covered the whole world." I got busy writing in my notebook.

Later that afternoon, we found the mountain road that led to Brian Head. We stopped in the small town there and asked a mechanic what could be done for our van's mountain troubles.

"The cars of the people who live here have been adjusted for high mountains. You could have your van adjusted—but that would be expensive, and you'd have to have it adjusted back when you leave. So you probably don't want to do that. The only thing you can do if it just won't go is to pull over and turn the engine off for a few minutes. When it cools down, it'll run better again." The mechanic wished us luck, and we left for the mountains.

Looking up the road, Mom asked, "Do you think the van will make it? It's steeper than any other road we've been up."

Dad shrugged. "All we can do is try. And pray."

I know I prayed. I'm sure they did too. But it wasn't long until the van began to slow down. Dad steered to the right side and kept going. Finally, we were just inching along. He pulled over at the next safe place.

"Well, here we sit until it cools down. Anyone else want a sandwich?" He opened the ice chest and began building a meal.

I explored around the road for a few minutes,

but I was bored and ready to go when he started the van again. We drove on for a mile or two, but soon we slowed down again.

"Dad, I think that bug is passing us. It might be time to stop," I suggested.

"Let's try to make it over this next hump," he replied. We just barely made it. And there below us was the town of Brian Head. Best of all, it was in a nice, almost flat meadow. We sputtered around until we found the place where we were staying.

Dad had a big surprise for us. We weren't going to be staying in a hotel room. Instead, our "room" was a whole apartment, with three bedrooms, a kitchen, and two bathrooms. Brian Head is a ski resort, and in the summers, they rent out the skiers' apartments.

"Dad, I love camping, but this is going to be a nice break. Hot showers every day, soft beds, and even cable TV! And hot meals three times a day." I was one happy camper. "Not that I didn't like what you cooked, Mom."

"It's OK, dear. I think I can get used to this place too." She looked very happy.

Later, we explored the rest of the building while Dad went to check in with his teachers. "Hey, Mom, look! A hot tub! Can we go swimming?"

"I'm sure we can spend a few minutes relaxing

when your father gets finished. Let's go back and change while we wait."

For once I'm writing at a nice desk under a good light. No raindrops or mosquitoes will be bothering me tonight! Tomorrow, Dad starts his field trips to find more evidence of Noah's flood. Of course, I'll be along to catch all the clues. So I'd better get to sleep. If I *can* sleep on a soft bed anymore. Well, all I can do is try!

Interesting Things I've Seen

Important Words

Paleontologists: Scientists who study bones and fossils to learn about animals or plants that lived long ago.

Fossils: Animals or plants—or parts of them—that have turned into rock.

Noah's Flood Clues

Dinosaur bones: Fossil dinosaur bones have been found all piled in one place by a lot of water. Very few plant fossils are found nearby, so the dinosaur bodies must have come from far away. This sounds like Noah's flood.

CHAPTER NINE

Whistling Woodchucks

Field trip
Cedar Breaks National Monument, Utah
July 16

It's been wonderful waking up in a dry, soft bed for a few days. And not having to pump the cookstove to make breakfast. I've even been able to catch up on my cartoon watching. But I'm glad that today is Dad's field trip to Cedar Breaks and that I get to go with him. I'm taking along my notebook in case I see something I need to write down.

"I think we should all go along on the trip," Mom had said at first. "It'll be fun."

"That's a great idea," Dad agreed. "It's only two miles from here, and the view is supposed to be beautiful from the cliffs. We're going to hike around the top of the—"

"Did you say cliffs?" Mom asked. "And you're going to walk along the edge? I think I'll stay here and rest, dear. You go ahead."

She grabbed Kayla and Alex to be sure that they weren't going. She almost grabbed me too, but I escaped with a promise to be careful. I left quickly in case she was thinking about changing her mind.

While I waited in the van, I found my cap and Dad's map, and by the time he got there, I was ready to roll. "Think the old van will make it?" I asked, patting the dashboard.

"Sure it will. Besides, it's only two miles away. We could always walk back." So we sputtered off behind the other cars. Soon we were parked at the first Cedar Breaks scenic overlook. We walked up to the edge with the other people from Dad's class and looked out over the cliff.

"Oooooh," everyone said.

One of the scientist-teachers started to explain. "The Cedar Breaks basin is more than 2,000 feet deep and three miles across." They call it a basin because it's bowl-shaped. It looks kind of like a football stadium with one end open. And we were standing on the top edge, where the highest seats would be. Except much, much higher.

It's hard to describe what Cedar Breaks looks like. From where we stood, we saw ridges of rock and deep canyons flowing toward the open end. The Cedar Breaks basin may look like a football stadium, but the rocky ridges look like lines of weird, lumpy, upside-down carrots. And these carrots have a lot of strange shapes. Some look like statues, some look like church steeples, and some are shaped like arches. (No, not like McDonald's. More like a horseshoe.) And they are all striped with dark red, light purple, and dull yellow.

"Wow," I said. "Mom's going to be sorry she missed this."

Dad agreed. "No wonder the Indians called this place 'the Circle of Painted Cliffs.' "

"Why do we call it Cedar Breaks? Are all the trees broken or something?"

"No," Dad laughed. "Early settlers got part of the name from the trees. Most of the trees here are a kind of cedar called juniper. But the second half of the name comes from the land. The settlers called this kind of land, with bare rocks and cliffs, *badlands* or *breaks*. That's how they got the name 'Cedar Breaks.' "

We followed the teacher down a path that ran along the top of the cliff but not too close to the edge. "What are we going to see, Dad?" I asked.

"We are going to see one of the oldest trees in the world."

"You mean a redwood tree?"

"No, that's the tallest kind of tree. The Great Basin bristlecone pine is the oldest," Dad said.

Just as we were stepping around a juniper log, I heard a sharp whistle. Who was that, I wondered. Then I heard it again. And I saw what was whistling. A short, fat animal was sitting right on the very edge of the cliff. Suddenly, it dropped out of sight!

"Dad, what kind of animal was that?" As I pointed, its head popped up over the cliff and it whistled again.

"That's a marmot. It's similar to a woodchuck. They whistle to warn each other of danger."

"Do they all live right on the edge of cliffs?"

"That's their favorite spot. I guess they feel safe there," he said.

We hiked out along one of the ridges toward a dead-looking tree. But up close, I could see some green branches. The teacher stopped and began to explain.

"This is the bristlecone pine. It looks almost dead, and the truth is, part of it is dead. But that's why the bristlecone pine lives so long. While one part dies, another part grows. So part of the tree is very old, and part is very young."

"How old is this tree?" someone asked.

"This one is more than 1,600 years old."

"Oooooh," everyone said.

"But other Great Basin bristlecone pine trees in the Southwest are probably more than 4,500 years old."

"Oooooh," everyone said again.

I walked up and touched the branches. It was hard to believe that this tree sprouted not long after Jesus' disciples lived. It was old when Columbus came to America! While I was walking around it, I saw another marmot near the cliff edge. I stepped slowly toward it to see how close I could get.

"Help! Oh, dear," I heard someone behind me say. I looked around to see what was the matter.

"I can't look. He's going to fall," the woman's voice said. I didn't see anyone in danger. Who is she talking about, I wondered.

"Zack, please come back up here," Dad said

quietly. "You're scaring that poor woman to death."

Me? She was worried about me? I wasn't even close to falling into the canyon. "Oh, brother," I said under my breath. "And I thought my mother was a worrywart."

Next we drove out into the countryside and stopped near a small mountain. The teacher led the group up to the top. I kind of dragged along behind, throwing rocks and kicking shells. All of a sudden, it hit me. Shells? I reached down and picked up a larger rock. It had seashells stuck in it.

"Hey, Dad," I called out. I had to run up the hill after him. "Look! What are seashells doing here?"

"That's what the teacher was just saying. This hill is covered with rocks and shells from the ocean. What do you think that means, Detective Zack?" he asked.

"That must mean that all this land was once covered with water," I answered.

"Yes. But it might not have been a mountain then."

"What do you mean?" I asked.

"Mountains like these are formed when the layers of rock far down inside the earth push up. It's hard to understand what those rocks down in the earth are doing. But they push up, and that forms mountains in long rows, like the Rocky Mountains we are in now."

"So this land could have been low and flat like the beach?"

"Yes, and scientists who believe in evolution might explain these shells by saying that this land was once at the bottom of the ocean."

"You mean this mountain used to be at the bottom of the ocean? And what's the bottom of the ocean now used to be the tops of some mountains?"

Dad nodded. "Scientists have found water-formed rocks and shells on mountains in countries all over the world. You can even find them on Mount Everest, the highest mountain in the world."

"Then," I said, "something must have turned this world inside out."

"If Noah's flood really happened, that's what you would expect to find," he replied. "That much water would have completely changed the earth. These mountains could have been pushed up during or after the Flood."

It's a good thing I brought my notebook. And a good pencil.

Interesting Things I've Seen

Two marmots

A very old tree (bristlecone pine)

Weird, lumpy rocks that look like upside-down carrots

Seashells on a mountain

Important Words

Basin: Bowl.

Breaks: A land of bare rocks and cliffs—also called badlands.

Marmot: A woodchuck that whistles and that lives in the mountains.

Bristlecone pine: The oldest trees in the world. Some are more than 4,500 years old.

Noah's Flood Clues

Seashells on mountains: Mountains all over the world have shells and water-formed rocks on them. And if some mountains were pushed up from the ocean floor, then something must have happened that completely changed the whole earth. I think it was Noah's flood.

CHAPTER TEN

Deep Canyon, Deep Trouble

Picnic trip
Zion National Park, Utah
July 18

"Are we going to church today, Daddy?" Alex asked, right after the blessing at breakfast.

"There aren't any churches around here," Kayla tried to answer.

"You're right, Kayla," Dad said, "but we're going anyway. We're going to one of God's most beautiful churches. We're going to take a picnic lunch and have church at Zion [zye-on] National Park."

"Where is that?" Alex asked.

"Oh, not too far away," Dad answered.

"Does it have big cliffs, like the place you and Zack went to the other day?" Kayla wanted to know.

"Even bigger," Dad promised. Then he saw the look on Mom's face. "But we're going to see them from the bottom of the canyon, not from the top."

"Are you sure the van will get us there?" Mom asked.

"Sure it will," he answered. "I hope."

Soon after starting we stopped at a crossroad. "OK, everyone, we have to decide here," Dad said. "There are two ways into Zion Canyon. The south road is pretty smooth and level and straight. But the east road winds down a curvy mountain trail and goes through a tunnel one mile long. Which one should we take?"

"Through the tunnel, through the tunnel," Alex, Kayla, and I shouted together.

"But it would take longer to get there," Dad warned.

"Tunnel! Tunnel!" we shouted again.

"But I might get carsick," he teased.

"Tunnel! Tunnel!"

"OK, OK," he laughed as he turned toward

the east road. Soon we were dropping down the twisting mountain road. It turned back and forth, back and forth, down toward the canyon. Many of the rocks here had strange shapes and bright colors too.

"Hey, Mom, look at that one. It looks like a red Christmas tree." I pointed out her window as I spoke.

"That's very nice, Zack," she said. She sounded funny. I looked at her more closely.

"Mom! You don't even have your eyes open."

"That's OK. Just tell me when we're at the bottom."

Soon we saw the dark mouth of the tunnel ahead. Dad turned on the headlights, and then we were swallowed up by the darkness. It did seem a little spooky to think that the mountain was on top of us. Especially when we couldn't see any light from either end of the tunnel.

But Mom seemed to like it. She even opened her eyes. "There aren't any bats in tunnels, are there?"

When we popped out into the sunshine of the canyon floor, everyone had their eyes wide open. The canyon was about as wide as a football field, and the walls went almost straight up on both sides. And I mean, they went a long way straight up.

A river flowed right through the middle, and beautiful green trees and grass grew on both sides. "Look," Kayla said, pointing out the window, "a deer. And there's another one." There they were, not afraid of the cars or people going by.

We explored for a while before lunch. "How far does this canyon go?" I asked Dad.

"Several miles. And farther on, it gets so narrow that you can reach across it and touch both sides. And in some places, the walls are almost 3,000 feet high."

After lunch, we sat together under a tree, next to the river, to have church. "We aren't having a sermon today. Let's just talk instead. Does anyone have an idea or a question we can discuss?"

I raised my hand. "Why do some scientists and teachers think the world is millions of years old? Are they just trying to trick us?"

Dad shook his head. "No, they're not trying to trick anyone. Many people, not just scientists and teachers, believe that the world is millions of years old. Some of them don't believe that there is a God, and some don't believe that the stories of Creation and the Flood in the Bible are true.

"Scientists have ways to measure how old rocks and things are. One way is called radiometric [ray-dee-o-met-rick] dating. It's hard to explain how they do it, but it tells them that many of the rocks and rock layers around here are millions of years old."

I was confused. "But how can they be right if the Bible is right?"

"There are two ways they could be right. How old was Adam when he was created, Kayla?" Dad asked.

Kayla said quickly, "One day old, of course."

"So he was a baby?" Mom asked.

"No, he was a grown-up. But he was only one day old. Right?"

Dad laughed. "It is kind of confusing. When God created Adam, He made him already grown up. It was just like Adam was already twenty or thirty years old. Maybe God did the same thing for the planet Earth."

"What do you mean?" Kayla asked.

"Maybe He created the world already old," I answered. "Could God do that, Dad?"

"I guess He could do anything He wanted. Maybe He created it like a planet millions of years old would be."

I got out my notebook to write. "What's the second way they could be right about the millions of years?"

"For that we need a Bible. Mom, did you bring

D.Z.S.N.F.—7

yours? I see that you did. Good. Let's let Alex read the first two verses of Genesis, the first two verses of the whole Bible."

Alex found it and read slowly. " 'In the beginning God created the heaven and the earth. And the earth was without form, and void; and darkness was upon the face of the deep. And the Spirit of God moved upon the face of the waters.' "

"Thank you, Alex. You read very well. Now, what do we know from those verses? Remember, God had not yet started the first day of creation. But what was already here?"

I thought about it. "Well, something was here. It was 'without form, and void,' whatever that means."

"That means that it was not shaped or finished, and nothing was on it. What else do the verses say?"

"The Spirit of God was here," Kayla added.

"Right. And what was He doing?"

Suddenly, the answer hit me like a cold shower. "Water! He was moving over the water—and God hadn't even started creating stuff yet."

"That's right, Zack," Dad said. "Before the week of Creation, the world was unfinished, but it was covered with water. Maybe it happened like this. Maybe when God began creating the universe,

He started with other parts of it and wasn't ready to work on the earth right away. So He rolled an extra blob of stuff over to one corner of space to wait—like you might roll a blob of Play-Doh to one side of the table until you were ready to work on it."

That made sense to me. "You're saying He waited to do the creating that Genesis talks about until the time was right."

"Exactly. So maybe the reason the rocks seem so old to scientists is that they really are millions of years old. Maybe they are part of the extra stuff God made the world out of."

Later, on the way back, we started having trouble. Yes, it was the van again. When we got to Cedar Breaks, it just wouldn't go any farther.

"Well, we'll wait here for it to cool down," Dad told Mom. "If it wasn't already dark, you could see down into the basin."

"That's OK. I don't mind," she said. "I wonder how long we'll have to wait. It's getting late."

We waited, but this time cooling off didn't help. The van moved out along the edge of the road, but it wouldn't go up the mountain. "I'll try and push while you drive," Dad told Mom as he got out.

"Do you think that's a good idea?" she asked, sliding into the driver's seat.

"It's the only idea I have left," he answered. He pushed on the back while Mom pushed on the gas pedal, but we still didn't go up the hill.

"I still have one idea," Mom said as he got back into the van. "Let's pray." And she did. "Father in heaven, please help us get back safely. Help us get our van over the mountain. Thank You, in Jesus' name. Amen."

We sat and waited. "If we could just make it over this last steep rise, we could coast down to Brian Head," Dad said.

I'm putting my notebook away for tonight. It looks like we are in deep trouble. Maybe it would help if I got out and pushed too. Or maybe we'll spend the night here on the side of the road.

Interesting Things I've Seen

A mile-long tunnel
Mule deer by the river
High, straight canyon walls

Important Words

Radiometric dating: A way scientists measure how old rocks and things are.
"Without form, and void": Not shaped or finished, and empty.

Noah's Flood Clues

An old earth: Scientists could be correct when they say that the world seems to be millions of years old. God might have created the world old, or He might have created it out of stuff He had made earlier, when He was working on other parts of the universe.

CHAPTER ELEVEN

Angels and Hoodoos

**Field trip
Bryce Canyon National Park, Utah
July 19**

I could have finished my cereal and toast. As usual, Dad rushed us out the door because we were going to be late; then we had to wait for him. So we sat in the van, waiting. And after last night, I'm not sure any of us wanted to get back into the van for another trip.

But Dad said he thought it'd be fine now. Of

course, that's what he said yesterday. And you know where that got us—stuck by the side of the road at Cedar Breaks in the middle of the night.

But what happened was pretty amazing.

In the few minutes after Mom had prayed for help, Dad and I tried pushing again. But that still didn't get us moving. Next we were going to open the hood and try to do something to the engine.

"Hey," Kayla called out from the back seat, "here comes a car."

From behind us, two headlights shone through the darkness. They came from an old, beat-up station wagon. It pulled over behind us on the side of the road, and two men got out. As they stepped into the beam of their headlights, I could see that they looked pretty beat-up too. They had old, dirty clothes and scruffy, dirty faces. I noticed that Mom leaned over and locked the van door.

"You folks got some kind of trouble?" The scruffy face produced a kind voice.

"Yes. Our van doesn't have enough power to get over this next rise. We're staying over in Brian Head, so if we could get over this last hump, we could coast in." Dad spoke in a friendly way as he explained. "Any chance you have a chain or rope that could pull us?"

The man looked over at his partner, who shook

his head. "No, I guess we don't. But we could push you if our bumpers match up."

"I don't think so. The bumpers on this minivan are probably higher than those on your station wagon."

"Let's try it and see," the man said and got into his station wagon. He pulled right up close behind us, until the bumpers were nearly touching.

"How about that! They are about the same height," Dad said. "Are you sure you want do this? If we move apart just a little and crash back together, it might damage your car."

"It'll be fine. Let's give it a try," the man said.

"OK," Dad replied. He got into the van, released the brakes, and put the shifter in neutral.

"Are you sure this is a good idea?" Mom asked.

"Even if it damages the bumper some, it won't cost that much. Not any more than it will cost to call a tow truck to come all the way out here. And this way we might get home tonight." As he spoke, I felt the station wagon bump the back, and then we were moving slowly up the hill.

We picked up speed as they pushed us faster. Then a little dip in the road made us move ahead of the station wagon. Dad slipped the car into gear and smashed the gas pedal to the floor. Nothing. The station wagon moved up from behind again.

"Hold on for a bump," Dad said. I grabbed Alex because he was looking back at the two men. The station wagon hit our bumper with a "thud," and then they were pushing us again. This time they stayed close to our van until we zipped over the top of the mountain.

"Here we go," Dad exclaimed. We pulled ahead of the station wagon and rolled down the slope.

"We're going to make it!" Mom said. I glanced back at the station wagon that was following at a distance. Alex was still staring at them. "I wish we could stop and thank them," Mom said.

"It wouldn't be smart to stop now. Besides, I don't remember any place to pull over until we get back to the town. When we get there, we'll stop to say thanks."

"They're gone," Alex said.

"What?"

"They're not there now. Their lights just went out." Alex was still looking back to where they had been.

"But they have to be. There was no place to turn, was there? And no houses where they could have stopped." I didn't understand.

Alex thought he did. "They must have been angels God sent to help us."

For a minute, no one said a word. My mouth

was hanging open like a flytrap. Then Mom said quietly, "Well, we did ask God for help."

When we were unloading the car, I saw Dad looking closely at the bumper. Then he looked up at me. "There's not a scratch or a dent," he said.

"Do you really think they were angels, Dad?"

"Well, it's kind of like the Flood story, Zack. You have to believe something. You can look at the evidence and decide that we were just lucky. They just happened to come along, and their car bumper just happened to match ours. We just got lucky when they bumped us and we didn't get a scratch. And they turned down some road we didn't see, or they turned around in the road and went back the way they came from.

"Or you can look at the same evidence and decide that whoever or whatever they were, God sent them along to help us."

Anyway, back to this morning. Dad finally made it to the van, and we followed the others in his class to Bryce Canyon. It's something like Cedar Breaks, only bigger and more colorful. And the rocks are in stranger shapes. One of Dad's teachers explained the view.

"Bryce Canyon is painted with more than sixty shades of red, pink, copper, and cream. And these strips of color seem to change as the sun moves across the sky. Some of the valleys between these colorful ridges are more than 1,000 feet deep."

He pointed at the rock shapes. "Some people see the forms of steeples, castles, or even animals in some of those strange shapes. But the really weird ones are called 'hoodoos.' "

"I think they look like castles," Mom said, with a dreamy look in her eyes. "Beautiful red-and-pink castles." I knew she would like the cliffs. But she did stay far back from the edge. To me, the formations all looked like hoodoos.

"What I want you to notice," the teacher went on, "is that cream-colored stripe near the top of the canyon wall. That layer of rock is found across four states. In some places it is pushed up in mountains. In other places it has been worn away by wind and rain. But that one layer of rock spreads out over more than 150,000 square miles."

"So what does that mean?" someone asked.

"The only place a layer like that could form today is at the bottom of the ocean. Only under water would there be similar conditions over that large an area. What I'm saying is that the best way to explain how such a large layer of rock was formed is—"

You guessed it. Noah's flood.

When we were on the way to our apartment,

Dad asked a question. "Zack, do you remember that floating stump we saw at the first campsite?"

I didn't remember. "Just a minute." I looked back in my notebook to the first few pages. And there it was, "one floating stump." I said, "I remember. We threw rocks at it. And we wondered if stumps always float straight up."

"Right. Do you remember what petrified wood is? That's wood that has turned to stone. Well, scientists were wondering about some petrified stumps they found in Yellowstone National Park. They were curious because so many were standing upright. Usually petrified trees are found fallen down, with their roots up in the air or broken off."

"And these stumps were all standing up like they were growing?" I asked.

"Yes," Dad said. "And scientists know they didn't turn to stone while they were still growing. So why are so many standing up straight?"

I knew this answer. "Because they were floating in water, like maybe in Noah's flood."

"That sounds like a good answer to me," Dad agreed.

That's why a good detective writes everything down. You never know when something strange will turn out to be an important clue.

Interesting Things I've Seen

"Hoodoos," or red-and-pink castles
Maybe two angels

Important Words

Petrified wood: Wood that has turned to stone, like a fossil.

Noah's Flood Clues

Big rock layers: Some layers of rock cover gigantic areas. Such large layers of rock could best be formed underwater. The best way to explain how that much land was underwater at the same time is Noah's flood.

Petrified stumps: Petrified stumps that are standing straight up could have been floating in the Flood until they settled into the mud.

CHAPTER TWELVE

Grand Canyon Clues

**Field trip
Grand Canyon National Park, Arizona
July 21**

"Dad, what did you do to fix the van?" I asked as I pulled out my notebook. We were almost to the Grand Canyon and were zipping right along. In fact, the van hadn't caused any problems for two days.

"Oh, I just opened the hood and adjusted a few things with a hammer," he said with a wink. "It wouldn't dare give us any trouble now." It didn't, and we were soon parking at the Grand Canyon.

I'll tell you this—the Grand Canyon is big. I thought the other canyons we saw were amazing, but this one makes them look like cracks in a sidewalk. One of Dad's teachers explained how big.

"From this side of the Grand Canyon, the North Rim, you can see all the way to the South Rim because it is only about ten miles away. In some places, the canyon is eighteen miles wide."

"Oooooh," everyone said.

"The Grand Canyon is 277 miles long. In some places, it is one mile deep. That green ribbon you can barely see at the bottom is the Colorado River. The stripes of color on the canyon walls show the different layers of rock under our feet. The layers were laid down, one on top of the other, like frosting on a chocolate cake. And it was done either over millions of years or by Noah's flood."

When he was finished, I just stood there, staring down at the river. One thing was for sure. It either took a lot of water or a long time to dig a hole that big.

"Hey, Zack," Dad called, "come over here. I want to show you something."

I ran to where he was standing, close to the

edge. "You see that thick brown stripe of rock on the canyon wall?"

I looked. "OK. What about it?"

"See the white stripe on top of it? See how the white stripe fits on top of the brown one smooth and flat, like a white cover on a book with brown pages?"

I used his binoculars to follow the two stripes as far as I could along the canyon wall. "Yes. So?"

"There are fifteen million years between them!"

"What?" I was lost. I didn't know what he was talking about.

"According to the ages scientists figure those layers of rock to be, after the brown layer was formed, fifteen million years went by before the white rock was laid on top of it."

"So?"

"Look how flat they are!"

I still didn't understand.

"Let me explain it this way," he said. "If I were going to make you a basketball court at home, I'd measure out a place, fix boards around it, and have it filled with wet cement. Then I'd smooth the cement until it was nice and flat and level."

"That sounds like a good idea. Let's do it when we get home," I said. He just shook his head and went on talking.

"Then we'd have to try to keep everything and everyone off it until it dried and got hard, right? Any person or dog or cat that walked across it would leave marks. Even leaves or sticks would leave dips and bumps in the cement."

"How long would it take to dry and turn hard?" I asked.

"Probably one or two days. But what if it took one or two weeks? Do you think we could keep everything off it?"

"Maybe," I said.

"But what if it rained? That might wash some of it away."

"But it might not rain for two weeks," I reminded him.

"OK. But what about one or two years? Could we keep it smooth for that long?"

"No way. It would have all kinds of tracks and humps and holes in it by then." I was sure about that.

So was Dad. "You're right. But think about those rock layers over there again. When the brown layer was laid down, it was soft for a while. And even after it was hard, rain and wind and sand would be wearing it down to make it rough and uneven."

"OK. And how long do they say it was lying

there before the white level was added on top?"

"Fifteen million years. Somehow it lay there for fifteen million years in the sun and the rain —and it was still nice and smooth and level when the white layer was formed on top."

"That doesn't make sense," I said. "It should have been worn down in lots of places by then."

"It makes a lot more sense to think that those two layers were laid down one right after the other when a big flood stirred up a lot of mud."

Later, on the drive back, Dad told me more about the rock layers. "Scientists try to figure how long ago an animal lived by where in the rock layers they find fossils of it. Remember that fossils are formed when an animal dies and is covered by sand or mud. Later, when that sand or mud turns into rock, the skeleton or shell turns to stone also. Or a fossil can be formed like the dinosaur footprints we saw in Texas."

"Like when a cat steps in wet cement and the footprint is there after it gets hard." I knew how that was. Bobby's driveway has cat footprints in it.

"Right. So when a scientist sees an animal fossil in a rock layer, he says, 'That rock layer was formed twenty million years ago, so that animal lived twenty million years ago too.' "

"That makes sense," I said.

"Maybe so," said Dad, "but listen to this. The most recent fossils scientists had found of what they called the tuatara [too-uh-ta-ruh], a reptile that looks like a lizard, were in rock layers they figured were 135 million years old. So they thought that the tuatara had died out 135 million years ago—until some living ones were found on a New Zealand island."

"Real, live ones?"

"Yes. And they looked almost the same as the fossil tuataras. So using fossils to decide how long ago an animal lived doesn't always work."

"If some animals living today look almost the same as their fossils, then either animals don't change much as time goes by or else not much time has gone by," I said.

"It's not hard for me to believe that they look the same today as they did before Noah's flood," Dad agreed. "In fact, I think it makes a lot of sense."

I was writing in my notebook when Alex spoke up. "Dad, I miss our dog, Murphy. Do you think he's OK?"

"You can find out yourself soon. We're leaving for home tomorrow."

"Are we driving straight home without stopping?" Kayla asked.

"No, we still have places to stop and things to see," Dad answered. "But we need to start on the road home. How about it, detective? Is the case nearly solved? Are we ready to go?"

I looked at my nearly full notebook. "Let's go home. I've got a lot to show someone about science and the Bible."

Interesting Things I've Seen

 A very, very big canyon
 Layers of rock that look like frosting on a cake
 A green-ribbon river

Important Words

 Fossil: What's left when a skeleton or body or the mud around a footprint turns to rock.
 Tuatara: A kind of reptile that looks the same as its "135-million-year-old" fossil relatives.

Noah's Flood Clues

 Living fossils: Either the tuatara reptile hasn't changed much in 135 million years or a lot less time has gone by.
 Smooth rock layers: How could they be so smooth and flat where they touch if they weren't both laid down at the same time?

CHAPTER THIRTEEN

The Case Is Closed

**On the freeway
Somewhere in West Virginia
July 25**

I'm not sure what woke me up, the screeching tires or the suitcase that fell on my head.

"What happened?" I pushed the suitcase off and tried to get up. We were stopped on the side of the road. Dad's door slammed as I sat up. He walked by my window to the back of the van.

Mom turned and smiled at me. "It's OK, Zack.

A deer ran out in front of us, but we swerved and missed him—I think. Kayla, are you OK?"

I pulled a sleeping bag away from the seat where Kayla was sleeping. "Kayla? Are you still there?"

Her sleepy voice came up from under her blanket. "Mom, tell Zack to stop pushing things on me. I'm trying to sleep."

I looked at Mom. She laughed. "I guess she's all right. Where's Alex? Is he OK?"

I looked over to where Alex was. He hadn't even stopped snoring. "He's still asleep, Mom." It takes more than almost crashing to wake him up. I guess little brothers are just like that.

Dad climbed back in. "We must have missed the deer. I don't see any sign of it or any marks on the van. It sure was close, though. I'm glad home is only two hours away."

For some reason, I didn't feel sleepy anymore. But Mom was yawning.

"Mom, if you're sleepy, I'll sit up there, and you can rest back here on the seat."

"Thanks, Zack. I am sleepy." She crawled back and I climbed over until we were settled.

The clock on the car radio said it was midnight. "Hey, buddy, be sure your seat belt is on," Dad said as I settled in with my notebook and pillow.

"So Detective Zack," he asked, "are you ready to close the case? Do you think the Bible story of the Flood is true?"

I looked at my notebook. "When you see the way the earth is put together, Noah's flood makes the most sense. With the rock layers and the deep canyons, the Bible has the best answer. You can look around and see clues everywhere that a big flood really happened."

"So what do you think Bobby will say? Will he believe the Flood story is true too?"

I waved my notebook around. "He has to! When I show him all these clues, he'll know I was right."

"Zack, what is the biggest difference between you and Bobby?" Dad stared ahead as he asked.

"Well, he is one inch taller than I. And we go to different schools and . . . I guess we believe different things."

"The biggest difference is that you've been raised to believe in God, and Bobby hasn't. He has always been taught that science and scientists have the answers to questions about where we came from and why we are here on earth."

"But his 'millions of years' idea doesn't fit all the clues! There are a lot of questions it can't answer. It has big problems." I was sure Bobby could see that.

"But what if a person doesn't believe in God?" Dad asked quietly.

I had to think about that for a while. The Flood was only possible if God made it happen. "I guess if you don't believe in God, evolution's millions of years is probably the best idea you'll find."

"I'm afraid you're right," Dad agreed. "But do you think Bobby will understand why you believe in Noah's flood?"

"I think so. At least he'll know that the Flood could have happened." I sat for a minute, watching the stars through the window. "Dad, why didn't God just give us proof that the Flood happened so everyone would know that the Bible is true? Wouldn't it be easier?"

"God built His whole universe around two things, Zack—love and freedom. He wants everyone to be free to choose what to believe. He loves them enough to let them choose," Dad explained. "He doesn't force anyone to believe. He just gives enough clues that anyone can have faith and believe if they choose to."

I was confused. "So I shouldn't try to show Bobby that the Flood is true?"

"Tell him about the clues you found. But don't worry about making him believe it. The most important thing to show Bobby is that God is real and that God loves him," Dad said.

"How can I do that?"

"By just being his friend and treating him with kindness," Dad answered. "And when you have a chance, tell him about God."

"And invite him to church once in a while?"

Dad nodded. "Sure. Now, why don't you get some sleep."

"OK. I just want to write a few more things in my notebook." I shined my flashlight on the last pages of my notebook so I could see to write.

It made sense that a flood that covered the whole world would leave some clues. You can't make a mess that big without leaving a mark! So I'm not surprised to learn that scientists have found flood clues.

I guess Dad's right. I believe all these clues point to Noah's flood because I believe in God. But when you add up all the clues, it's easy to believe what the Bible says. I'm glad I know the truth, and I'm glad I know that God loves me. It's nice to know that He doesn't force anyone to believe. He lets me make up my own mind.

I guess God is just like that.

Wait a minute. My flashlight batteries are going dead again! Should I ask Dad for more? No, I'll wait and finish this tomorrow.

Interesting Things I've Seen

I've seen that compared to the Bible, evolution's millions-of-years idea is pretty weak.

I've seen that the most important thing is finding out that God is real and that He loves us.

Important Words

Love: What God has for everyone.

Freedom: You get to choose for yourself what to believe.

Noah's Flood Clues

My conclusion: The clues don't prove that Noah's flood really happened, but seeing all the evidence makes me believe it did.

Dad, I need more batteries again. But there's no hurry—unless we're going on another trip soon!

DETECTIVE ZACK

and the Mystery at Thunder Mountain

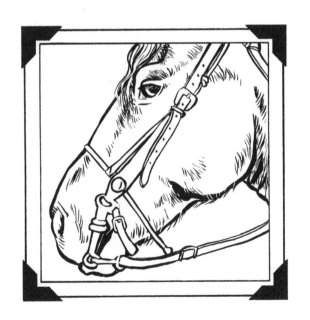

Dedication

To those who knew me before I was "anybody" in writing, and whose encouragement helped change that:

Aileen Andres Sox
(who published my first children's story),
Chris Blake,
Barbara Jackson-Hall,
Richard Coffen,
Kermit Netteburg,
Cec Murphey,
Elaine Grove,
and my brother, David.

At least now, everyone will know who to blame.

Contents

CHAPTER ONE

Thunder Mountain Camp

Day One

A pencil doesn't make a very good fly swatter. I've been trying to swat a mosquito with this one, but I keep missing.

I'm lying in one of the top bunks of the Cherokee cabin at Thunder Mountain Camp. Writing in this cabin while the other guys are shouting and throwing pillows isn't easy, I can tell you.

While I was unrolling my sleeping bag, Luke, one of the other Cherokees, climbed up on the next bunk. "Is this your first year at Thunder Mountain Camp?" He went on before I could answer. "I was here last year. We had a great time."

I like Luke already. He laughs a lot. "What are

the horses like? My mom signed me up for horse-back riding, and I'm not sure I like horses," I said.

Before he could answer, there was a loud smack against the other side of the wall. Then we heard loud, rude laughing. "What are they doing in there, tearing up the bunkbeds for firewood?" Luke asked. He threw his hands up and shook his dark black hair. "Those Mohawks! I knew they would be trouble as soon as I saw them."

"Who?" I asked, as the hooting and shouting next door continued.

Peter, who was unrolling his sleeping bag on another bunk, explained, "The Mohawks are the other half of this camp house. Every camp house has two cabins." He counted on his fingers as he talked. "The Cherokees and the Mohawks, the Comanches and Arapaho, the Hopi and the Sioux, and the rest."

Max joined us at my bunk. "And the Mohawks are the worst of the bunch. Did you know they already broke a light in the bathroom, ran one of the Arapaho's hats up the flagpole, and teased one of the Hopi girls so much she wants to go home?"

"Who are those guys?" I asked. No one had an answer for that. But Peter had another question.

"Isn't it time to eat yet?" Just then, the dinner

bell started bonging. Peter was the first one to the door.

The food looked good. Peter's plate was piled high. We sat at a table with some of the Hopi girls, including my sister, Kayla. Pastor Mike asked the blessing and then we dove in.

"Oh, yuck!" A voice called out over the noise of the cafeteria. We all turned to see a tall kid with red hair staring at the food in the serving line. "You call this food?"

Kayla slapped her fork down into her mashed potatoes. Gravy splattered on Luke, but she didn't notice. "That guy makes me so mad!" she said, with clenched teeth. She pointed her fork at me. "He's the one who made Holli cry."

I helped Luke wipe the gravy off his arm. "What did he do that was so mean?" I asked.

Kayla's friend, Ally, answered. "He heard her name when she arrived. After her parents were gone, he started saying, 'Hopi Holli! Dopey, Hopi Holli! Are all the Hopi's as dopey as you?'"

Luke and I just looked at her. "OK," she finally added, "I know it sounds silly to you, but this is her first time away from home, and she was already scared."

Suddenly, a loud whistle almost broke our eardrums. Everyone turned to look. "Attention, campers." It was Mrs. Carter, the camp director. "Welcome to Thunder Mountain Camp. This week is going to be full of fun. You're going to learn to do things you've always wanted to do. But more importantly, you're going to learn more about God."

I was glad to hear that. Because I have questions about God.

Mrs. Carter went on. "You're going to find that the counselors are here to help you learn and have fun. And you already know how good the food is!"

"Yaay!" Some of the kids cheered and clapped. Kayla looked at me. "It's not as good as Mom's food," she whispered.

"Booo!" It was the red-haired boy and his friends. Mrs. Carter looked at them and said, "I'd like you all to meet someone. Mr. Morgan, please come out and say hello to the campers."

The door to the kitchen swung out. A man stepped up and ducked through the doorway. A big black beard covered most of his face, and the black hair on his head stuck out from under his hat. The whole cafeteria got very quiet.

"Campers, I'd like you to meet Mr. Morgan. He's our camp cook." Mr. Morgan waved at us with a long butcher knife and grunted.

Mrs. Carter spoke again. "Mr. Morgan only has two rules about his food. Would you share those with us?"

Mr. Morgan stood up straighter. His head nearly touched the wooden beams. "Number One," he growled, "take all you want, but eat all you take. Number Two, don't complain about it. If you don't like it, just don't eat it." He stared around the room for a minute, then stalked back into the kitchen.

Red-hair and his friends sunk halfway under their table. Kayla took another bite and whispered, "I like this food fine."

Mrs. Carter went on. "You'll be taking classes in horseback riding, canoeing, swimming, tracks and trails, and crafts. Also, each cabin will be performing a scene from the Bible at campfire. Your counselors will be explaining more about this later."

Campfire that evening didn't last long because they knew that everyone needed to get settled and get to sleep. Luke and I were tiptoeing back from the bathroom, trying to walk silently like real Indians did. We froze when the door of the Mohawk cabin flew open. Alan, one of the Mohawks, stuck his head out. "Where is the [he used a curse word] trash can, anyway?" he grumbled.

Then he just dumped the trash on the ground.

Back at our side of the cabin, we had some questions for our counselor, Dave. "What are those Mohawks doing at this camp?"

Dave stretched his tall body across two of the bunks and pretended to get comfortable. He closed his eyes and asked, "What makes you think they don't belong here?"

Everyone tried to talk at once. "They are rude and mean!"

"I heard them cussing."

"I saw cigarettes in one of their bags."

"Cody told me he's been in jail before. He said he burned down a building."

"He was lying. He always lies."

Dave sat up and waved his arms until we stopped. "So you don't think they fit in at a Christian camp?"

"No way!" Luke answered for all of us.

Just then, thunder crashed outside. Only, it wasn't raining. In fact, the stars and moon were shining brightly. "What was that?" Dave asked. He jumped to the door and looked out. We rushed to the windows.

"It sounded like it came from down there," Luke said, pointing into the darkness, "down by the cafeteria."

"I'll be back," Dave said. "You guys stay in the cabin," he called as he disappeared.

"What do you think it was?" Luke whispered.

I had been thinking about that. "Our trash cans at home make noise like that when you crash them together. But why would someone be getting in the trash?"

While we waited for Dave, I was thinking about what he said. About the Mohawks. It reminded me of why I'm writing in my notebook this time.

It all started when I got back from my trip to Egypt and Israel. I had two notebooks full of clues about the Bible and stuff, and . . .

"What'cha writin'?" Luke asked.

Before I could answer, every light in the camp went out.

CHAPTER TWO

Mystery in the Dark

Day Two

It was completely dark. I mean, there was no light anywhere. I waved my hand in front of my eyes, and I couldn't see it. For a second, everyone was silent. Then everyone was talking.

"What's going on?"

"Ouch! I hit my head."

"Get off me!"

"Wait," I shouted. "Everyone stand still. Luke, isn't your flashlight hooked to your belt?"

"Oh, yeah." We could hear Luke fumbling with the light. Then we heard another sound. A stick snapped right outside the door!

"What was that?" Luke whispered. Everyone else was silent again. Then we heard the door creaking open.

"Turn on your light," I hissed at Luke. But

15

before he did, a voice spoke.

"Hey, are you guys OK?" It was Dave.

We hit him with pillows and questions. "What are you doing sneaking in on us?"

Max sounded tough. "Are you trying to get hurt?"

Before he could tell us anything, the lights came back on. "All right, let's get back to our bunks," Dave announced. "That's enough excitement for one evening."

Max called out from his corner. "So, what was that noise?"

"Yeah, what is going on?" Peter asked. He seemed really worried about the cafeteria.

Dave shook his head. "Some of the trash cans were knocked over. And then for no reason, someone pulled the switch that shuts off electricity to the camp lights."

I started thinking like a detective. "How many people know where that switch is?" I asked.

Dave's eyebrows went up for a second. Then he shrugged. "Who knows? We'll worry about it tomorrow. Now, let's hit the sack."

"Don't you mean the bag?" Luke asked. "You know, the sleeping bags?" Everyone groaned. Max threw a pillow at him.

"But you didn't finish telling us about those

Mohawks," Brian reminded Dave.

Dave nodded. "When everyone is in bed, I'll go on." He waited for a few seconds while Luke emptied three rocks, two sticks of gum, and two quarters out of his pockets.

"OK," Dave said, sitting down beside Brian, "they aren't Christians. Those guys are from a big city. They have never been to a camp. I'm not sure they've ever been to a church! But every summer, we like to bring in kids who especially need the chance to spend time out in nature. And a chance to learn something about God."

We couldn't argue with that. They definitely needed some kind of help.

"Anyway," Dave went on, "they'll learn about horses and canoes and stuff. But a lot of what they learn will depend on you guys."

"What?" I asked.

"A lot of what they learn about Christianity will come from watching Christians—you guys, the counselors, everyone here who claims to be a friend of Jesus."

That gave me a lot to think about. That's kind of what this notebook's all about this time. Last year, I didn't get to go to camp because my dad had to go to a class out in Utah, and the whole family went along. Of course, I learned a lot

17

about Noah's flood on that trip.

My friend, Bobby, thought that the story of Noah's flood and all the stories of the Bible were just fairy tales. But when I told him all the clues I had found on our trip to Utah, he said, "OK. Maybe the flood really did happen."

And when I told him about the things I saw on my trip to Egypt and Israel with Dad and Dr. Doone, he was impressed. He said, "Wow! Maybe the stories in the Bible are true. And God really does help people." He seemed happy to know that.

But the next day, he wasn't smiling. "I talked to my dad about the Bible being true and everything," he told me. "Dad said, 'Ha! Most of the trouble I have at the shop is with Christians. (His dad fixes cars.) They're always trying to cheat me out of my money. If the Bible is true, then people who say they believe in it should be good people. And from what I've seen, they aren't.' "

I didn't know what to say. I think Bobby's dad is right. If the Bible is true, then people who believe in it ought to be different from people who don't. They ought to be more kind and caring. Believing in God should change the way they act.

So, this summer, I'm going to watch for clues that Christians really do act differently. Or clues that they don't.

I was still thinking about all that when I fell asleep. The next thing I knew, someone was screaming in my ear!

I jumped up, but it was just barely light, and everyone else was still asleep. Just when I decided it must have been a dream, it happened again.

"Screeeak!" It was a blue jay sitting in a tree right outside my window.

"Go away!" I said. Then I covered my head with my pillow. I guess I went back to sleep. The next thing I heard was a trumpet.

Really, it was a recording coming from the loudspeaker at the cafeteria. I crawled farther down into my sleeping bag.

A voice followed the trumpet. "Good morning, campers. It's time to rise and shine!"

"It's still nighttime," a voice from Luke's bed said. "I don't want to get up with the chickens."

The loudspeaker voice continued. "Fall out for flag raising in forty minutes."

"Why must we get up so early?" a voice asked.

"You heard Dave last night," I mumbled. "We have to stand at the flagpole and say the pledge of allegiance before breakfast."

"Breakfast! Did someone say breakfast?" Peter swung out of his bunk and snapped on the lights.

"Let's get rolling, Cherokees."

After that, there was no use trying to sleep. While we were getting dressed, Luke started searching around his bed. "Where's my money?" he asked. "I know I had two quarters last night. I put them right here with my gum and rocks."

"I remember seeing them," Brian said. We all did. But now, they were gone.

Luke spun around and looked at all of us. "All right, funny joke. Now, who's got my quarters?"

Everyone shook their heads. Luke rolled his eyes. "So someone snuck in here in the middle of the night and stole my two quarters? I don't think so. I think one of you has them."

Just then, the Mohawks walked past our windows, shouting at each other. Cody's red hair was waving in a friendly way as if it were trying to make up for the scowl on his unfriendly face. "I think it was one of them," Brian whispered.

"Maybe you're right," Luke said with a frown. None of us liked the idea of Mohawks sneaking into our cabin at night. "Come on," he sighed, "let's go before we're late."

I left the cabin last, and took a close look at the door. Could someone sneak in? I guess so! The door didn't even have a lock on it! I started working on a plan.

Clues About Christians

If the Bible is true, then people who believe in it ought to be different from people who don't. They ought to be kinder and more caring. Believing in God ought to change the way people act.

Thunder Mountain Mystery Clues

Some people were out running around the camp. They knocked down the cafe trash cans.

For some reason, the camp lights were all switched off.

Someone snuck into our cabin and took two quarters.

CHAPTER THREE

Mohawk Trouble

Day Two

At the flagpole, we found out that we were supposed to do more than just stand there. We had to stand in line, at attention! Mrs. Carter made us wait that way until everyone was standing properly.

Of course, it was the Mohawks who took so long. "What is this, the army?" Cody grumbled.

Then the Navahos raised the flag. I'm sure the red, white, and blue looked awesome up in the early morning sky. But with all that bright morning light, I had a hard time getting my eyes open far enough to see.

"Hi, guys!" Kayla bounced up and plopped her tray onto our table at breakfast. I grunted at her. Ally sat down too. She stared at me.

"When does your brother wake up?" she asked

Kayla. Like I wasn't even there.

"Usually by lunch time," Kayla laughed.

"Cut the funny stuff, girls," I said. "We've got problems." I told them about our night at the cabin. About the trash cans.

"We heard that noise too," Kayla said.

"And what happened to the lights?" Ally asked.

"We don't know. I want to look around for clues today," I said. "But I don't know when. I've got horse class, then crafts, then canoeing. Maybe I'll have time after supper."

Ally sighed. "I want to look too. But the Hopi cabin is on kitchen duty this morning. That means we have to clean up this mess." She stabbed the eggs on her plate.

"And we get to work with that delightful, happy, smiling Mr. Morgan," Kayla added. Almost as if he had heard her, Mr. Morgan stepped out of the kitchen and glanced around the dining room. Scowling, he went back inside.

"We'd better hurry back for inspection," Luke reminded me. "The others are already gone."

"See you later," I said to the girls after swallowing the last of my orange juice, "maybe at supper." On the way up the hill, I was thinking about Mr. Morgan. Why was he so grumpy and mean-sounding? If he was supposed to be a Christian, he sure didn't act much like one.

As we got close to the cabin, we heard shouting. "Look at this mess! I'm not cleaning it up. It's their trash."

Max, Peter, and Brian were standing in our cabin yard. In front of them on the ground were candy bar and gum wrappers, a banana peel, and some other papers. Max was still shouting.

"We already cleaned up our side of the cabin yard. Then we went in to make our bunks. Now look at this!"

Luke nudged me. "Isn't that the trash Alan was dumping out on the ground last night?"

I nodded. "They pushed all their trash over to our side of the yard, so we would have to pick it up."

"Well, we're not going to do it," Max declared. "We'll just push it back."

A voice called from the corner of the building. "Hey, keep your trash out of our yard." Cody, Alan, and two other Mohawks were standing there.

Max went right over to them. "You know this is not our trash. We know you put it on our side. Now pick it up, or we'll just throw it all back."

"We're not touching it. And anyone who throws trash in our yard gets it." He punched his hand with his fist in case anyone didn't understand what they would get.

Luke spoke up. "Let's just get Dave and tell him what they did. Then they will be the ones who fail inspection."

I was trying to decide whether to go with Max's idea or Luke's when I saw what Brian was doing. He was picking up the trash.

Max saw him too. "Brian! It's not our trash."

"We don't have to pick it up," Luke added.

Brian looked at us. "Remember what Dave said last night?" he said quietly. "About them?" He nodded toward the Mohawks.

I understood what he meant. About the Mohawks not being Christians. And watching the rest of us. And what they would learn.

I started helping Brian pick up trash.

Cody said, "Good idea, Brain."

"His name is Brian," I stated.

Cody laughed. "Whatever. Just keep your trash out of our yard." The Mohawks disappeared around the corner, but we could hear them laughing.

Max was so mad he was shaking. But he took some deep breaths and started helping. So did Luke. Max said, "Being a Christian is harder than I thought."

My first class this morning was the horse class. Mom had told me some long name for it, but I figured the point was learning to ride a horse. Luke and I were walking by the Hopi cabin on our way to the corral when Kayla and Ally ran out.

"Hurry up," Kayla shouted. "Or we'll be late for the horses."

I didn't really think the horses would care, but we ran with them. We got to the corral in time to hear Bob, the horse trainer, tell everyone that the class was called horsemanship. "First, we will learn to saddle a horse. Then we'll see about mounting and directing them at a walk."

I nudged Luke. "Look who's here." It was Cody and Alan, looking like they thought horses were as boring as homework.

"First," Bob said to the group, "I'll introduce the horses. This little brown beauty is named Petunia. She's gentle and careful and dependable." He turned to a giant red horse. "This is Tiny."

Everyone laughed. "I'd hate to see what you call big," Luke shouted.

Bob laughed too. "You can see that Tiny was named before he grew up. He's gentle also." The next horse was jet black. "This is Blackjack. He's smart and fast and frisky. He knows all the tricks for getting rid of a rider. Don't get him going unless you know how to handle him."

He introduced the other horses. "Today we'll

begin to learn how to saddle and care for our horses. And if we have time, we'll hop on and take a short ride."

Bob and some of the other helpers showed us how to toss on the blanket first, then the saddle. I didn't like standing almost underneath Tiny to buckle it on.

"Get it good and tight," Bob warned, "or you'll find yourself riding on the side of the horse. On your way to the ground."

Finally, we were ready to try a short ride. Bob sat on his horse, a palomino named Paint, and showed everyone how to work the horse's gas pedal and brake with the reins. "No matter what you've seen on TV, never kick your horse in the flanks to make it go. You direct a horse left or right by pulling on that side of the reins. Now, how many of you have ridden a horse before?"

He started matching kids with horses they could handle. "I hope I get Blackjack," a voice whispered behind me. It was Ally. "I like horses. I ride them every chance I get."

"I haven't ridden much," I said. "I'll be happy with Petunia. Or maybe a nice fence post. My mom wanted me to sign up for the special riding class after supper, but it was full."

"I knew it would be," she smiled, "that's why

I signed up for it early."

Bob was helping campers get up on the horses' backs. He called it "mounting the saddle," and he wanted it done correctly. "Put your left foot in the stirrup, then set up and swing your right foot over. Then hold the reins until I say otherwise."

"Rats," Ally said as Bob helped Alan up on Blackjack. "I wonder if he's really ridden a lot like he said." She got another black horse, and I had no trouble getting up on Petunia.

"Today, there will be no running," Bob called from Paint. "We're just learning to walk. Use the reins to direct your horse, and stay in line."

As we started down the path, I followed Ally's horse. I heard Alan, ahead of us, making fun of Cody's horse. "What kind of nag is that? It looks old enough to die before we get back."

Cody didn't like it. "What good was it to give you that fast horse? You've never even been on a horse. If you were any good, you'd be at the front of the line."

Alan couldn't take that. "I'll show you. Watch this!" He kicked Blackjack with both heels.

"Whaanahehe!" Blackjack bolted straight up on his hind legs, then dropped down and took off like a shot. Alan was holding on for his life.

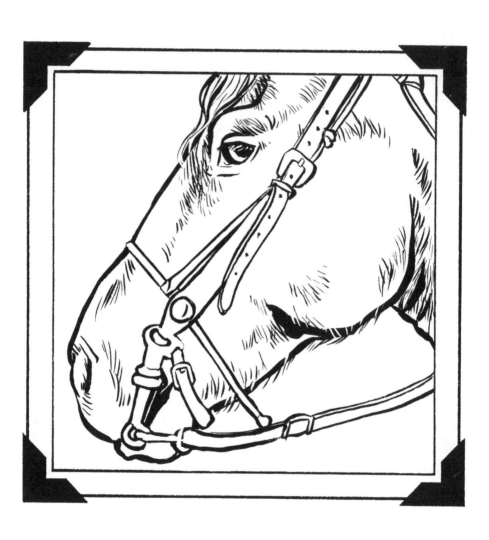

CHAPTER FOUR

Danger at the Corral!

Day Two

When Blackjack hit high gear, he flashed past the other horses like they were standing still. Alan was barely hanging on, bouncing from side to side in the saddle. Paint took off after them, almost before Bob clicked the reins and leaned forward.

Ally pulled up beside me. Her face was white. "They'll never catch Blackjack. Bob said he was the fastest horse here."

I don't think they would have. But Blackjack did something no one expected. Especially not Alan.

Blackjack stopped.

Alan flew over Blackjack's head and disappeared in the cloud of dust. Then Blackjack reared up! His hooves flashed in the air over Alan's head!

Suddenly, Paint was there. Bob jumped off and walked directly in front of Blackjack. He ignored the flying hooves and talked softly. "It's OK, boy. Settle down, now. Everything is all right." Bob protected Alan from Blackjack's hooves with his own body.

Alan didn't move. As Blackjack began to calm down, only tossing his head and whinnying loudly, Bob walked him back to the corral. There, he patted him a few more times, then turned him loose inside the fence. He whistled for Paint and motioned for Alan to come back in. "What happened?" he asked when Alan arrived.

"I didn't do anything," Alan started to say. Ally almost jumped out of her saddle.

"Not anything? Then why did the horse run?" Bob asked.

"Well, maybe I kicked him a little," Alan mumbled.

Bob went through the roof. Well, he would have, if there had been a roof! "You kicked him? After what I said? No, you probably weren't even listening. Do you know that that horse could have killed you?" By now, Bob was right in Alan's face.

Alan stared at the ground. The rest of us looked away like we were actually trying to decide if it would rain. I felt bad for Alan, even though Bob was right and Alan deserved it.

The rest of the class went by very quietly. Alan got another horse—a sway-backed old nag that probably hadn't run since the year Alan was born.

At supper, Mr. Morgan walked by our table. He glared at Luke, who had three hot dogs on his plate. "I'm eating them, sir," Luke said, stuffing a whole hot dog in his mouth at once.

Some people couldn't do that. Luke did it, and never stopped talking. It was amazing to see. And gross.

But seeing Mr. Morgan reminded Kayla of something. "Zack! Something strange happened in the kitchen this morning. Ally, you tell him."

She talked between bites. "I was cleaning out the big serving pans—you know, the ones that hold the biscuits and stuff that never got served. Anyway, I started to dump them in a trash can, but Mr. Morgan stopped me."

Kayla interrupted. "Stopped her? He shouted and got all huffy and told her to go on and sort the silverware." She waved a carrot stick around as she talked.

Ally ducked away from the swinging carrot and went on. "Right, and here's the strange part. He took those leftovers and dumped them in another trash can."

I shrugged. "So he's picky about his garbage."

"That's not the really strange part!" Ally stopped and waved a forkful of broccoli at me. "Will you let me finish?" She tapped my plate with the fork until the broccoli almost came off.

"OK, I'll listen. Just get that stuff away from me. Broccoli and I have this understanding. It doesn't eat me, I don't eat it."

"Sorry," she said. "This is the really strange part. He put the trash can in the refrigerator!"

Now, that was weird.

"Anyway," Ally sniffed, "I thought you might want to know. After all, that noise last night had something to do with trash cans, didn't it?"

"Yes. Of course. Thank you." I tried to be specially nice. Ally is the kind of girl who keeps her eyes open. The way things were going, I might need her help. Besides, I didn't want any more broccoli attacks. "Be sure to let me know if you see anything else suspicious."

She smiled. "I will."

Luke shook his head. "Putting garbage in the fridge is a very strange thing to do. What do you think it means?"

"I don't know," I answered. "What we have so far is this: garbage cans knocked around at night. Someone switching off the electricity. Money missing in our cabin. And the cook keeping garbage cans in the refrigerator."

"What can all of those things mean?" Kayla asked.

"I don't know," I said. "Only one thing we can know for sure—someone is outside at night doing something. And whoever it was came into our cabin and stole Luke's money."

"I know who my first suspects are," Luke said, rolling his eyes toward the Mohawk table.

"Or maybe that strange Mr. Morgan," Ally added.

Just then, Mrs. Carter blew her whistle. With his hands over his ears, Luke said, "I wish someone would steal that thing."

Mrs. Carter talked about camp spirit and made announcements. "Tomorrow, the Arapahos pick up the trash, the Zuni cabin will help clean up after breakfast, the Comanches have the flag-raising and lunch clean up, and the Cherokees help after supper."

There was a low moan from Luke and Max.

"The next day we'll begin our hiking trips to the overnight camps. Your counselors will be telling you more about them. Before you go, Wrangler Bob wants to say something."

Bob looked smaller as he stood in the cafe than he did in the corral. And he didn't seem dusty enough. He cleared his throat and began. "Most of you have probably heard about our problem with a runaway horse this afternoon."

He waited while those who hadn't heard whispered questions to their friends. Then he went on. "Blackjack bolted because an inexperienced rider kicked him. We were very fortunate that no one was hurt. And it's a good lesson to all of us."

He turned toward Alan's table. Alan looked like he wanted to slide under his chair. "But I'm not here to talk about riding. I'm here to apologize to Alan."

If Alan's jaw fell open any more than mine did, it must have hit the table.

"I lost my temper this afternoon and yelled at Alan in front of everyone, so it's only right that I apologize in front of everyone. Alan made a mistake, a bad decision, and I was right to correct him. But it's never right to yell at someone after they know what they did was wrong."

The whole room was silent.

"Being a Christian means treating people like Jesus would, and I didn't do that this afternoon. I'm sorry, Alan, and I hope you'll forgive me."

A small voice came from Alan's table. "OK."

I thought what Bob did to save Alan from Blackjack was really something. But apologizing to him in front of everyone was really amazing!

Still, I guess Bob was right. Being a Christian means treating people like Jesus would. And Bob sure did that tonight.

I grabbed Luke's arm. "We're going to have to hurry to get set up before campfire."

Luke looked at me like I was crazy. "Get what set up?"

I wriggled my eyebrows. "No one's sneaking into our cabin tonight. We're going to set a trap!"

Clues About Christians

Bob risked his life to save Alan from Blackjack. That seems like a very Christian thing to do.

But apologizing to him was really treating him like Jesus would. Bob seems like someone who is different because he believes the Bible.

Thunder Mountain Mystery Clues

The cook is keeping some garbage cans in the refrigerator. Why would he do that?

CHAPTER FIVE

Petunia and the Good Samaritan

Day Two

"We need to catch whoever is coming into our cabin," I told Luke. "There may be a connection to the other mystery at the cafe."

"What will we do?" Luke asked. "Stay up all night and watch for them?"

"We can't do that," I said as we walked into the cabin. "That's why we have to set a trap." Max, Peter, and Brian crowded around.

"What trap?"

"What are we going to catch?"

I waved my arms. "Hold on, everyone. We have to think this through." I paced back and forth. "We know that someone came in during the night and took Luke's money. And the only way in here

41

is through the door."

"Why couldn't they come through the windows?" Peter asked.

"The windows all have screens," I pointed out. "And the screens are latched from the inside. Even if the latch wasn't fastened, whoever crawled in would have to crawl across either your bed or Max's. Without waking you up."

"No way," Max said. Peter shook his head too. I went on.

"So whoever it was, came in through the door. And whoever was out there last night was probably at the cafe too."

I went over and opened the door, pulling it toward me. "What we need is something to wake us up if someone pushes the door open."

"What if we just block the door so it can't be opened," Brian suggested. "We could move Peter's bed in front of it."

"That would keep them out," I agreed, "but we wouldn't know who was doing it. Or if they had something to do with the kitchen mystery."

It was quiet for a moment. Then an idea hit me like a hammer. "Peter! You have soda pop in your suitcase, don't you?"

Peter nodded. "I used to have six cans. But now they're all empty."

"But do you still have the cans?" I asked.

Peter looked confused. "Of course. I collect them for recycling. I'm taking them home."

"Perfect!" I shut the door. "We'll take Peter's cans and stack them here in front of the door. Whenever the door opens, the cans will fall over, and the noise will wake us all up."

"Good plan!" Max shouted. Peter started digging the cans out of his stuff. I stacked them six-high, right next to the door.

"This is gonna be great," Luke said. "Nobody's gettin' in here again. I'll leave all my quarters out now." He waved a clinking little leather bag around.

"How many quarters do you have?" Peter asked. We all gathered around to look in his money bag. It was stuffed!

"Why would you bring so many quarters to camp?" Brian asked.

Luke looked down. "I thought there might be video games."

We were still laughing about that when the cans crashed over behind us.

"Whoa! They're here!" Max shouted, jumping for his bed.

"My quarters! They're after my quarters!" Luke cried. He crawled under his bed.

"What is going on?" Dave called from the doorway. "What are these cans doing here?"

"Dave," I sighed, collapsing on Luke's bed, "you scared us half to death."

"I can see that." He laughed as Luke crawled out. "But what are you doing?"

We told him about it—how Luke's money was taken, how we were setting a trap, and how we were going to catch the thief.

"Well, those cans will certainly tell you if someone opens the door. But don't you think that anyone who is trying to sneak in will hear the cans crash? And run?"

I hadn't thought of that. There would be no way to wake up and get out the door in time to catch them.

"Anyway," Dave said, "it's almost time for campfire. Let's not be late." We followed him down to the campfire bowl. I was still thinking about the trap. But the program gave me something else to think about.

After a few of our favorite loud songs, Mrs. Carter welcomed us all to campfire. "Are you having fun so far this week?"

"Yeeesss!" everyone shouted. The Mohawks didn't shout, but they were smiling.

"There is still a lot of excitement to go. Tomorrow, the first of the cabins will go on their over-night hike to Mountain Treehouse Camp." While she talked, the bushes behind her rustled suspiciously. We heard whispering.

Suddenly, off to one side, a kid in a wraparound robe-thing stepped out of the bushes. "Whoops," he said as he realized it wasn't time for him to show up. Everyone laughed.

Mrs. Carter went on. "I see they're ready. Tonight, the Arapahos have our program. They will be doing their skit, 'The Good Samaritan.'"

Greg, the Arapaho counselor, stood up. "It's important to remember that Jesus told the story of the Good Samaritan to answer a question: 'What do I really have to do to be a follower of God?'"

Greg left, and the same kid came back out of the bushes and walked by in front of us, whistling to himself and watching the sky as if he didn't have a care in the world. Suddenly, two guys rushed out, grabbed him, and threw him to the ground.

One of the Mohawks whispered, "Yeah! Why don't we get to do fun parts like that?"

The two robbers grabbed the traveler's bag, beat him with it, and then left him there, lying in the dirt.

Before long, someone all dressed up like a priest

came out. He looked at the body lying there and sniffed. "Someone really should help the man. I can't because I'm on my way to church." Then he hurried away.

Another Arapaho came out. He stopped to look at the traveler. "I'd better get out of here fast! Whoever did this might still be around. I'll report it to the police in Jericho."

Then someone walked by the front carrying a sign that read, "What we would expect the Samaritan to do."

Then Bob, the horseman, rode out of the bushes on Paint. He stopped when he saw the boy lying on the ground. Then he laughed and shouted, "Good! Another dirty Jew got what he deserved." He threw something at the body and laughed again. Then he rode away.

The sign boy came back. This time the sign said, "What the Good Samaritan did."

When he was gone, the Arapaho counselor came out of the bushes, riding Petunia. When he saw the traveler's body on the ground, he stopped and picked him up and put him on the horse.

"Oof," the boy grunted when he was thrown across Petunia's saddle. Everyone laughed when Petunia turned her head to look at him like she was saying, "Are you all right?"

They took him to a place by the fire where he was cared for. At the end of the skit, Pastor Mike came up. "So Jesus asked, 'Who was that man's neighbor? Who truly cared about him?'"

"Petunia did," someone called out.

Pastor Mike laughed. "You saw what the Samaritan could have done. The Jewish man was his enemy. But he was a true follower of God—not like those who pretended to be followers by doing religious things."

He looked around at each of us. "What I want this skit to teach you is that being a follower of God will make you different. It will make you care about everyone, not just your buddies or cabin mates."

I've been thinking about how people should be different if they are real Christians. But I haven't thought about myself. Am I a real follower of God? Or am I just pretending?

Clues About Christians

The Good Samaritan was good because he was a follower of God. That made him act differently than other Samaritans would act.

Thunder Mountain Mystery Clues

A trap will catch the sneaky thief. If we can figure one out.

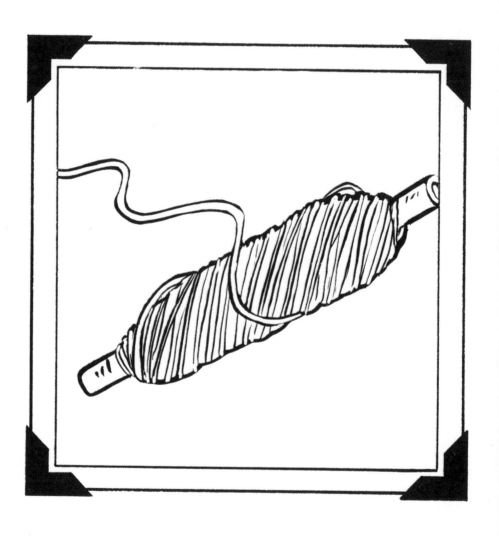

CHAPTER SIX

Trapped!

Day Three

You'll never believe what happened last night. "You know the problem," I told the guys. "We need to wake up when someone opens the door, but do it quietly so we don't scare them off, right?"

"Right," they agreed.

"Luke, didn't you tell me your mother made you pack a kite?"

"Yes," he grumbled, "she thought this might be a good place to fly a kite. I tried to tell her it was in a forest."

"But did she pack in some kite string?" I asked.

"Yeah. A big roll of it. You want it?"

I nodded. "I have a plan." Luke gave me the string. "Peter, lie down on your bed like you were sleeping." He laid down with his arms behind his head.

"Now, take off your shoes." Peter looked at me, but untied his shoes and dropped them on the floor. "And your socks."

When his socks were off, I demonstrated my plan. "See, I tie a string to the doorknob like this. Then, I tie the other end of that string to Peter's toe. Like so." I looped it around the big toe of his right foot.

"So when the door opens, it pulls his toe. And he wakes up!" Max was catching on.

Peter wasn't so sure. "How hard would it pull? Would it hurt?"

"I'm sure whoever opens the door will open it slowly," I answered. "And we'll tie one of those slip knots the way we learned in crafts today. You know, the kind the teacher told us not to make because they would just slip apart."

"Yeah," Luke agreed, "every one I made yesterday came apart. That's why the wallet-thing I'm making looks like spaghetti."

"Let's try it," I said. While Peter lay still, I opened the door slowly. The string tightened and pulled, then came loose from his toe.

"It works!" Peter said. "I would have woken up for sure."

Brian wasn't convinced yet. "But then what happens? What does Peter do if someone comes in and he wakes up?"

"Yeah." Peter suddenly frowned. "If I shout, whoever it is will run out."

I snapped my fingers. "Of course! We'll set up a tug system."

"A tug what?" Max asked, scratching his head.

"A tug system," I explained. "We'll tie a string from Peter to you, then one from you up to Brian."

Luke caught on. "Then a string goes from Brian to you and then one down to me. It's a great idea!"

"Maybe you'd better say it again," Max said. "Why do we all need to be tied down with strings?"

"Not tied down," I said, "tied together. See? When the door opens, it wakes Peter. He pulls on his other string to wake you up."

"Then I'll pull on my string and wake Brian up." Max was getting it. "And Brian's string will wake you and then Luke."

We agreed that when Peter felt the tug, he would pass it on, then count to ten. Then he would hit the light switch. We would all jump up and face the thief together.

It was kind of weird going to sleep with strings on two fingers. This time, we waited until Dave was in bed before we set our trap. So when a tug woke me up later, I knew the trap was sprung.

I laid there with my eyes closed, smiling. Because I was sure that the guys were all awake, just waiting for Peter to flip on the light. Then finally, we would have our thief.

But I didn't hear any other noises, and the light didn't come on. Finally, I sat up and found two problems with my plan.

First, no one was awake. Second, I could tell no one was awake because it was already getting light. I lifted my hand to look at the string and wonder what went wrong.

"Hey, stop pulling my arm," Luke mumbled. I leaned over to look and that woke up Brian.

"What? Who's . . . what?" Brian woke up slowly. He rubbed his eyes, which pulled on Max's string. Max woke up a little and stretched. That yanked Peter's hand.

"Yeow!" Peter cried. Without opening his eyes, he sat straight up and flipped on the lights. The rest of us just blinked at him. Finally, his eyes opened. "Did we get 'em?" he asked hopefully.

Max groaned and rolled over. Or tried to. His string got tangled in his bed frame. Luke tried to get up, but his string got caught on the sleeping bag's zipper. On the other side of the room, Dave woke up and looked at us.

"You look like something a spider drug in," he said. "Let me guess. Another trap?" We nodded.

"Well, I can see who it caught."

Max ripped the string off his finger and threw it at me. "The next time you have a bright idea, go fly a kite!"

When the trumpets got us up later, Dave said, "Hey, have you guys seen my watch? You know, my silver Mickey Mouse watch? I'm sure I left it right here by my bed."

So not only was my trap a real flop, but somehow, someone got in and took Dave's watch. It was a disaster of a morning. And guess who was all bright and cheery at breakfast.

"Isn't this a beautiful morning?" Kayla said as she sat down. "I wish every day started just like this."

I tried not to hit her with my fork.

"Did you hear about the horses?" Ally asked. "Bob thinks someone was in the corral last night. He thinks someone may have been riding Blackjack."

"Well, we know it wasn't Alan anyway," Luke laughed. "I don't think he'll get anywhere near Blackjack."

Kayla shook her head. "Don't be too sure about that. I heard that Alan is taking those special riding lessons every evening after supper."

"No way!" I said. "I know there weren't any

more openings for lessons. I wanted to sign up, but they were full. You're taking those lessons, Ally. There wasn't any room left, was there?"

Ally stared at her food. "No, there wasn't."

"Bob said the only way anyone else could take lessons was if someone dropped out." I stabbed my hash browns. "And I'm sure no one would do that."

Ally didn't say anything. But Kayla did.

"Didn't you tell me last night that you quit those lessons?" she asked Ally.

Ally looked at her and then at me. "OK. I told Bob I would drop out of the special riding class if Alan wanted to take it."

"Why?" I asked. "You told me how much you like riding. And how much you don't like the Mohawks."

Ally shrugged her shoulders. "I already know how to ride. He probably never had the chance to learn." I just looked at her. "So I was trying to be nice," she said. "So sue me!" Then she threw her toast at me.

I didn't say anything, but I was impressed. She gave up horse-riding just to help someone else. Someone she didn't even like. It kind of reminded me of the Good Samaritan.

Then I remembered why we were talking about horses in the first place. "Why does Bob think someone was in the corral last night?" I asked.

"Blackjack was out in the field instead of in the corral. I guess Bob doesn't think Blackjack could get out there without some help," Kayla answered.

I slapped my hand on the table. "We'll go there right after supper to look for clues."

"No, we won't," Luke said, through a mouthful of eggs. "We have cleanup duty after supper."

I was afraid that we wouldn't get to work on any clues today. Boy, was I wrong.

Clues About Christians

Ally showed that a Christian who believes what the Bible teaches really will be kind to people who aren't nice.

Thunder Mountain Mystery Clues

Our trap was a flop.

Dave's watch was taken from our cabin last night.

Someone may have been messing with the horses last night.

CHAPTER SEVEN

Tracks and Trails

Day Three

"What do these tracks tell you?"

Luke bent down close to the ground. "I don't hear anything."

Cindy laughed. "OK, smart guy, out of the way."

Cindy is our teacher for the track-and-trails class. "In this class, we will learn to identify animal tracks and trails in the wild," she told us. "We will also learn about marking a trail for someone else to follow."

She took us out to the lake and pointed out some tracks on the shore. "Even though Luke can't hear them, these tracks do tell us a lot. These are the tracks of a raccoon. You can see that he walked into the water here, then came back to the shore."

We followed the trail of the raccoon along the shore as Cindy told us more about tracking animals. "You can often read a whole story from the tracks. But you have to look closely, and pay attention to what you see."

She pointed to a set of smaller tracks away from the water. "What can you tell about this animal?"

I looked closely. "Well, it's a small animal. It had little claws that dug into the sand."

"And what does this mark tell you?" she asked, pointing to a line that sometimes showed in the sand between the footprints.

I thought about different small animals and how they walked. Then it hit me. "It's a tail! The animal had a long tail that sometimes dragged on the ground behind it."

"Right," Cindy said. "These are the tracks of a wood rat, or pack rat, as it's sometimes called. Now look, see how the tracks change here?"

Brian bent down this time. "The claws are digging in deeper. The back part of the footprint is missing. It started running. The front of its feet dug in deeper, like ours do when we run."

"I wonder what it was running from," Max said. "Maybe the raccoon?"

"No," Cindy stated, "the raccoon wouldn't be hunting a rat. Let's follow the tracks and see if we can learn anything else." We followed her, bent low to look at the tracks. Suddenly, she stopped.

Luke bumped into her. I bumped into Luke. Max bumped into . . . well, you get the picture.

"Ow!"

"Watch it!"

"Wait!" Cindy held out her hand. "Look at this!"

We poked our heads out past her arm and stared at the ground. There were more tracks and marks, but I couldn't tell anything from it.

"All the tracks are messed up," Max said. "You can't tell anything from that."

"Don't be too sure," Cindy said with a smile. "Look closely, and pay attention to what you see."

I looked again. The rat's tracks were headed straight toward a patch of briers. He was trying to get away, but from what? There were no other tracks beside his.

I looked at Cindy. She smiled but said nothing.

Right before the briers, the tracks were messed up. The dirt was kind of dug up, like someone had scratched it up with a stick. What could chase a rat without leaving tracks but scratch up the dirt? I tried to picture it in my mind. Suddenly, it snapped in place like I had pushed a button on the TV remote and found the right channel.

"It was a bird! An owl, I bet!"

Cindy clapped her hands. "Exactly! Probably a great horned owl. Look at this—the rat was running for his life here," she pointed to the tracks, "and here the owl struck. See where his claws raked the ground?"

Everyone got close and followed her story.

"But the owl missed. See where its wings beat the ground here? And here?"

We could see how the dirt was brushed back.

"And look at this. These leaves and twigs on the brier bush were broken. The owl must have been angry about missing dinner and pounded at the bush with its wings."

I let out a breath I didn't know I was holding. We all looked around as if the owl might be lurking in a tree nearby, still in a bad mood.

Cindy stood and looked at us all. "See what you can learn when you pay attention to what you see?"

Boy, did I!

That night, at supper, we told Kayla and Ally about the owl and the other things Cindy had taught us. "She told us how to mark a trail so someone could follow."

"What do you do, carve an arrow in a tree?" Ally asked.

"No, that might damage the tree," Luke explained. "You can show the way to go by using sticks—like this." He stuck the end of his knife into his mashed potatoes and then leaned it between the tines of his fork. "See? That points the direction of the trail."

Kayla said, "I see," and shuddered as Luke licked the mashed potatoes off his knife.

"Or," Luke went on, "you can mark the trail with rocks. A little rock on top of a big rock"—he put a green pea on top of the mashed potatoes—"means the trail goes straight. If the trail turns, you put another rock on the side it turns toward." He put another pea on the right side of his potatoes, as if his trail was turning toward Kayla.

"Let's go," I said. "We get to help clean up tonight."

"Ug," Luke grunted. "What's our hurry?"

I slapped his back. "Clues, man, clues. We're going to pay attention to everything we see in that kitchen tonight."

Kayla pointed to Luke's plate. "You'd better clean your plate. I wouldn't want to be in your shoes if Mr. Morgan sees you throwing away good food."

Luke glanced around like he was really afraid, then began stuffing everything into his mouth at once. The girls said, "Ooh, yuck!" and left quickly. I went to the kitchen.

"I'm here to help," I called as I opened the door.

Mr. Morgan said, "You can start on the pots. Spray them off in the sink. Then we'll run them through the dishwasher."

I tried to keep an eye on everything while I washed. I noticed one thing quickly. While Mr. Morgan wasn't exactly friendly, he wasn't mean either. When someone didn't understand, he explained it carefully until they did. He didn't shout or make fun of anyone. I guess I was expecting him to be different.

"See anything yet?" Luke whispered as he went by carrying a bag of trash.

"Not yet," I answered. "I'm trying to watch what happens to the leftover food. Look!"

Someone had started to empty the food pans, and Mr. Morgan stepped up. "I'll take care of that. You get the broom, and start sweeping the dining room."

I raised my eyebrows and nodded at Luke. I would keep watching. But, wouldn't you know it, I got busy spraying one big pot, and when I looked again, the food pans were gone.

When my pots were done, I saw Mr. Morgan helping a kid stacking plates for the dishwasher. *This is my chance*, I thought. I walked back toward the refrigerator and looked around. *That extra food must be around here somewhere.*

Then I heard something strange. It was a knocking sound, but it seemed very far away. I moved toward it. The noise was coming from the refrigerator. It sounded like someone was locked inside!

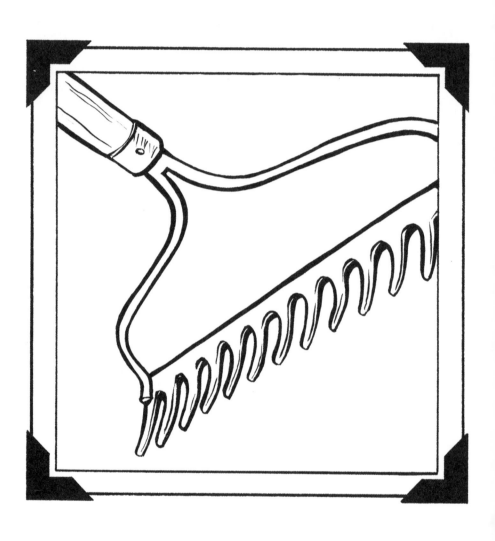

CHAPTER EIGHT

Clues in the Sand

Day Three

I grabbed the handle and swung the door open. There, next to the big can of potato salad, was Luke!

"T-t-thanks," he said through chattering teeth. He rubbed his arms to get warm. "The door locked behind me. I thought I was stuck for the night."

I looked at the inside of the door. "Did you push the handle release button?" I asked.

"What? I tried to push the handle, but it wouldn't go down."

I pointed to the sign on the door that said in big red letters: "Push Handle Release Button to Open Door." An arrow pointed to a big red button.

Luke just stared. "Oh. I guess I didn't see that."

I grabbed his cold arm. "Let's get out of here before Mr. Morgan shows up." We ducked out the back door of the kitchen and sat in the sun. Once we were outside, I asked the question I had been saving. "What were you doing in the refrigerator, anyway?"

Luke sniffed. "I saw Mr. Morgan carry some garbage bags in there. So I waited until he was gone, then snuck in to see what was in the bags."

"So? What was it?"

He kicked at the sand under our feet. "I don't know. As soon as the door shut, I forgot about the bags. Now we'll never know."

The sand gave me an idea. "Maybe we can still find out something. Come on; let's go ask Mrs. Carter for a rake."

We found Mrs. Carter at the camp office. "What can I do for you, gentlemen?" she asked.

"Can we borrow a rake?" I asked. "We want to do a specially good job of cleaning around our cabin tonight."

"Certainly you can. I like to see campers who take an interest in keeping their areas clean. Take one of the rakes leaning against the back of this building. You will bring it back tomorrow, won't you?"

"Yes, ma'am," I answered. We found a rake next to some cement blocks and dashed back. Everyone was gone by then. The cafe was dark, and the back door was locked. The evening's trash cans were lined up along the back wall. "Perfect!"

"Are we through running yet?" Luke asked, still panting.

I laughed. "We are ready to set our trap." I got busy. "I'm going to rake the sand in front of the door and trash cans all nice and smooth. That way, whoever comes here during the night will leave clues behind."

Luke was catching on. "Footprints! They'll leave footprints, and we'll be able to track them."

"Exactly," I answered. Soon, the ground was ready to collect clues, and we were ready to go.

"Wait a minute," Luke said as we headed back, "you told Mrs. Carter that we were going to rake around our cabin."

I grinned at him. "We are. That's the other half of our trap. We'll rake around our side of the cabin and around the Mohawks' side."

"That sounds like a lot of work."

"But look, this way we get clues on both mysteries. We'll know if the Mohawks leave their cabin. And we'll know if they come to our side."

Luke began to see the plan. "By the footprints. Right!"

I went on. "And the bonus is, if their footprints at the cabin match footprints going to the cafe, we'll know who's been down there too."

Luke was ready to dance a jig. "I like it! I can't wait to tell the guys."

I grabbed his arm. "Let's not tell them. After the way the last trap worked, I'd rather wait until we catch someone." He agreed to keep it a secret.

When we got to the cabin, the Cherokees were in an uproar.

"It happened again!" Max shouted.

"What?" I tried to ask. "What happened?"

Brian answered. "Some of Max's money was stolen. He left it on the floor while we went to supper, and now it's gone."

Max stopped stomping around and explained. "After swimming, I stopped by the camp store and bought these granola bars. My change was three dollar bills and a fifty-cent piece. I've never had one of those before, so I was going to keep it."

"So where is it?" Luke asked.

"I was late for supper, so I ran up here to change. I just left my money on the floor by Brian's bed. When I got back after cleanup, this was all that was left!" He waved the three dollars in our faces.

Something seemed strange to me. "Why would someone come into our cabin, steal fifty cents, and leave three dollars?"

"I was wondering that too," Brian said. "If

someone was looking for money, they'd take it all. Wouldn't they?"

Luke told everyone we were going to rake outside to get a head start on tomorrow's inspection. And that was true. Our cabin would look great with the yards all raked smooth. We took turns raking a wide section of the dirt around our side. When we started raking in front of the Mohawk side, their door opened.

"What are you doing?" Cody asked. For once, his voice didn't sound mean, just curious.

"We're raking," I answered.

Luke added, "Just trying to be neat and clean."

Cody didn't believe that. "You in some kind of trouble? And this is your punishment?"

"No," I answered. "We're getting a head start on inspection tomorrow."

"Then why are you raking our side?"

"Just trying to be friendly?" Luke suggested.

For a minute, I was afraid he would catch on to our plan and tell us to leave their side alone. But he rolled his eyes and went back inside.

"We'll have to be the last ones in tonight, so we can smooth out the last footprints after campfire," I whispered as we finished.

Luke smacked his forehead with his hand. "Campfire! The Hopis are doing tonight's skit.

Hurry, or we're going to be late!"

The Hopis did the story of Zacchaeus. Kayla was dressed up in a rich purple robe. At her house, by the front row of benches, there was a table set with a white tablecloth and glass dishes. She strutted around, taking money from other Hopis who were sitting on the ground, eating from old paper plates and dressed in dirty old clothes.

Then someone walked by, wearing a big sign around her neck. It was Kayla's friend Holli. The sign read "Jesus is coming!" Kayla's eyes got really big, the way they do when she sees a spider. She paced back and forth as if she didn't know what to do. Then she started to go to her right. Holli tapped her on the shoulder and turned around. A sign on her back read, "No, that way!" and pointed to the left.

We laughed.

A crowd of people (really, it was four or five Zunis who were helping the Hopis) came out of the woods from the left. Kayla rushed up to join them, but somehow, she was always behind them. They were taller, so she kept trying to jump up and see past them.

Finally, she gave up and ran to a tree. Climbing up to the first branch (not too easy in a robe), she sat and waited. Soon, someone in a white robe, wearing a fake brown beard, walked up and stopped under the tree.

I wasn't sure who it was until I heard her voice. "Zacchaeus, come down. I'm going to your house for dinner." It was Ally!

They went to sit at the table with the white cloth and pretended to eat. Kayla pretended to listen, while Ally pretended to talk. Pastor Mike stood up to speak.

"We're not sure what Jesus said to Zacchaeus, but the Bible tells us that Zacchaeus changed. That same night, he offered to give half of all he owned to the poor and to repay the people he had cheated with four times as much."

Kayla got up and took bags of paper money to the poor people still sitting on the ground. She threw handfuls in the air, and they grabbed for it.

Pastor Mike went on. "Zacchaeus wasn't rich anymore, but now he was happy. One thing always happens when a person decides to become a follower of Jesus. That person is always happier. And more fun to be around."

I'd never thought of it that way.

On the way back to the cabin, Luke grabbed my arm. I almost dropped my flashlight. "Trouble!" he hissed as he pointed.

I looked. There was a light on in the kitchen!

CHAPTER NINE

Confusing Clues

Day Four

"Quick! Let's go." Luke and I raced toward the cafe as fast as we could in the dim light of dusk. I didn't turn on my flashlight. We circled around to the back side and tried to peek in the kitchen windows.

"It's Mrs. Carter," Luke whispered. We could see her walking through the kitchen.

"What is she doing?" I wondered out loud. She seemed to be looking for something. "Hey, maybe she thinks something strange is going on too."

The light clicked off. I ducked down behind a bush. "Quick, get down. She'll see us."

"Not my dark skin," Luke whispered as he watched the back door open.

"Lucky," I muttered from the ground. Mrs. Carter stepped out with her flashlight shining around at the trash cans. She stood still for a moment, then walked away toward the camp office.

"We'd better go to the cabin and get the rake," Luke said.

"Wait, let's look first." I turned on my flashlight and traced Mrs. Carter's steps through the sand.

"Only one set of footprints," Luke said.

"She must have come in through the cafeteria doors," I said. "Look, her shoe print is kind of small, and it has crisscross lines. We'll know which prints are hers tomorrow morning."

Back at the cabin, we made a last-minute trip to the bathroom so we would be the last ones in for the night. I raked the last prints from in front of the Mohawks' door very carefully. And quietly.

"How are we going to wake up before everyone else?" Luke whispered when the lights were out.

"Don't worry. I have a plan," I whispered back. I wasn't worried. Every morning of camp so far, my blue jay friend had returned to shriek at the top of his beak. I don't know about anyone else, but it woke me up every time. Before, I wasn't happy about being woken up at sunrise, but this time, it was going to work out fine.

"Screeeak!" My blue-feathered alarm clock was right on time. I hopped down and woke up Luke. "Let's go," I whispered.

We snuck out the door just as the sun was coming up. "Walk out away from the cabin so we don't mess up any tracks," I reminded him. We circled our side.

"I don't see anything," Luke said after a minute.

"Wait, here's something." I bent down and looked close. "It's a wood rat's tracks, just like the ones we saw yesterday. How about that! A wood rat visited our cabin."

"We don't have time for rats," Luke hissed. "Let's go around to the Mohawk side."

There, in the smooth dirt, were two sets of footprints, leading away from the door. Obviously, two people had left that cabin. I looked at Luke. "Paydirt. Quick, to the cafeteria."

What we found there was a complete surprise. "What on earth are those?" Luke asked. I knelt down to look closer. Mrs. Carter's prints were still there, but leading up to the door was something else, something bigger.

"They're horse tracks!" I exclaimed. "Look, they go right up to the door. The horse was walking slowly. See? The tracks are very clear. The sand around them is not disturbed much. Wait a minute, I've found more footprints."

We looked closer. "Someone got off the horse and walked to the door," Luke pointed out.

"Are those footprints the same as the ones at the Mohawk cabin?" I asked.

"I can't remember for sure. Let's go back and see," Luke said. "We'd better hurry. People are starting to get up."

Before we got to the cabin, I heard a door slam. I knew we were sunk when I heard Cody's voice. "Come on, guys. Let's get the showers first."

When we got there, the dirt in front of their door was stomped on by at least four pairs of bare feet. The shoe prints were gone.

"Rats," Luke said. "Well, at least we still have the prints down there."

I looked past him to the milk delivery truck coming up the road. "Not for long, we don't." We watched while it backed up to the kitchen door, destroying all the tracks there.

It was a big disappointment after all our trouble. Still, we had found an important clue. And something else we saw was tickling the back of my mind, but I couldn't quite remember what.

We did get a perfect score on our inspection anyway.

At horse class, we followed a new trail. As we walked our horses through the woods, I pulled Petunia up beside Ally. She was on Blackjack this time. I said, "Riding horses isn't so bad. It's easier than riding a camel."

Ally's eyebrows crawled to the top of her forehead. "A camel?"

"I'd rather ride Petunia than Old Beauty any day," I said, remembering the knobby-kneed humpback my friend Achmed and I rode. "On camels you go up and down and back and forth. It gets old fast. And then when they run! Ouch!"

Ally just stared. "You know how to ride a camel? And you're afraid of horses?"

I sat up straight. "I am not afraid of horses. I just prefer smaller animals—ones with less teeth and hooves. By the way, Bob was right about someone riding the horses at night."

"How do you know that?" she asked.

I told her about the tracks at the kitchen. "Someone rode a horse to the door and went in. I don't know what they're doing, but they're using a horse to do it."

"Have you told Bob?" Ally asked.

"No. I want to find out what's going on first."

We stopped the horses near a stream and got off to let them drink. "Hey, Zack," Ally called, "look over there." She pointed across the stream.

It looked like a big blue tent. "Why would a tent be out there by that farmer's field?" I asked. "Let's ask Bob."

When we asked him, Bob looked over at the tent and frowned. "I understand that a family lives there," he said.

"All the time?" I asked.

"In a tent?" Ally added.

He sighed. "The story is that they were homeless, and the farmer lets them live on the land while they work for him."

"Well, that's nice," Ally said.

Bob snorted. "I don't think the farmer is doing it to be nice. The camp gave them that old tent. Before that, they were living in their car. I think the farmer treats them like slaves. And he calls himself a Christian."

"Why don't you report him to the sheriff?" I asked.

He frowned again. "Then the family wouldn't have anywhere to live. Besides, Mrs. Carter has offered to help them, but they're too proud. They don't want our help."

Ally and I walked back to the bank of the stream. I was showing her animal tracks in the mud, but there weren't many that the horses hadn't trampled. We walked farther upstream.

There weren't as many horse tracks there, but one I recognized. "You can sure tell where Tiny has stepped," I laughed. "He's the only one big enough to make that print."

Ally looked around. "Zack, Tiny didn't come on this ride. He's back at the corral."

"Are you sure?" I looked around too. "He isn't here. But that has to be his print. Doesn't it?" I looked again. "It could look bigger because of the mud. Or maybe he was here last night."

Ally looked shocked. "Was it Tiny's tracks by the cafe?"

"I'm not positive. There were big tracks, but without other tracks to compare with, I'm not sure how big. But what if those homeless people are stealing things from the camp and using Tiny to haul them back here?"

Ally looked a little scared. "We'd better tell Bob."

"No," I decided. "Those people have enough trouble without us accusing them of being thieves if they aren't. Let's wait until we have proof."

When we got back to the camp, Luke was waiting. "Something else was stolen last night. Brian's silver whistle is missing."

Clues About Christians

If a person says "I am a Christian" and then treats people like that farmer treats those homeless people, then, either the Bible isn't true—or else that person isn't really a Christian.

Thunder Mountain Mystery Clues

Someone is using the horses to do whatever he or she is doing. The hoofprints by the cafe prove that.

We saw a hoofprint that might have been Tiny's out by the stream. Could the homeless people be stealing food and using Tiny to haul it?

Two sets of tracks left the Mohawk cabin during the night.

No footprints led to our door. But Brian's silver whistle disappeared anyway.

CHAPTER TEN

Tracking Down a Thief

Day Four

At supper, Luke and I sat with Kayla and Ally at the corner table. We wanted to discuss the mystery without other people overhearing us.

"First things first," Ally said. "What do we think is going on?"

Luke answered. "We think someone is stealing things—from the kitchen and from our cabin."

"I've heard about the missing things from the cabin. Is anything missing from the cafe?" Ally asked.

That puzzled me too. "I haven't heard of anything," I said, "but Mrs. Carter was searching around last night. And Mr. Morgan acts suspicious of everyone. It could be that things are missing, but they aren't telling us."

"Someone has been down here twice," I said. "The first time, when they knocked over the trash cans and then when they turned out the lights . . ."

"How'd they do that, anyway?" Luke asked.

"The breaker switches for the electricity are in that shed over there," I said, pointing to a small building between the cafe and the office. "Dave told me that's where they had to go to turn them back on."

I went back to what I was saying. "The second time was last night. We saw the footprints and hoofprints."

"We also saw footprints coming out of the Mohawks' cabin," Luke said.

"And don't forget the hoofprint at the stream," I added.

Ally started counting on her fingers. "So our suspects are the Mohawks, Mr. Morgan, or those homeless people."

I sighed. "Or it could be someone we haven't thought of."

"It does leave a lot of questions with no answers," Kayla agreed. "Like, is anything really missing from the cafe?"

"And, why would Mr. Morgan take anything?

He doesn't want any little thing to be wasted."
Ally wondered.

"And, why are things missing only from our
cabin?" I asked.

Luke had to join in. "And, why don't we ever
get ice cream for dessert?" We glared at him. He
ducked down like we might throw things. "Well?
Don't you wonder about that?"

Ally ignored him. "Are you sure nothing is
missing from other cabins?"

I nodded. "I haven't heard of any. And what
has been taken from us and what hasn't is very
strange."

"What do you mean?"

While Luke explained about Max's fifty-cent
piece being taken and his three dollars left, the
back of my mind started tickling again. I thought
about what had been taken—the coins, the watch,
the whistle. Something about it . . .

"That is weird," Kayla was saying.

"It's like someone is starting a collection," Luke
agreed.

Click. "That's it!" I shouted.

"What'd I say?" Luke ducked down again.

I grabbed him. "Luke, get the Cherokees together at the cabin. I'll meet you there in ten
minutes."

Ally asked Kayla, "Does your brother get like this often?"

I didn't bother with them. I ran to find Cindy.

Ten minutes later, all the Cherokees and Dave arrived at the cabin. Kayla and Ally came too. Cindy, our tracking teacher, and I were waiting. "We've all been wondering who's been taking our stuff from the cabin," I said. "Well, I found the thief."

"Cindy took our stuff?" Luke asked.

"Shh!" everyone said.

I went on. "I figured it out when I realized what all the missing things had in common. They were all shiny."

Now everyone thought I had lost my mind. Except Brian. I could see the wheels turning in his head. "If you've got it all figured out, where is the stuff?" Max asked.

"Follow me," I said. We walked back behind the cabin to the edge of the woods. I stopped at a skinny old stump and looked at Cindy. She nodded. I kicked the stump over with one blow.

There, in a pile of leaves and bark, was a watch, two quarters, one fifty-cent piece, and a silver whistle.

"What? How?"

As the others grabbed their stuff, Brian figured

it out. "It was a pack rat—a wood rat—wasn't it? They like shiny stuff."

"That's right." I grinned. "Luke and I found its tracks this morning in the dirt by the cabin. When I figured out what was happening, I asked Cindy to help me track it back to its home."

"Way to keep your eyes open, Zack," Cindy said.

"That was great!" Max added. "No wonder our trap didn't work. We should've had a rat trap."

Dave laughed while he slipped on his watch. "So he was sneaking in every night and taking the shiny stuff. Good detective work, Zack."

Ally didn't say anything. But she looked impressed.

Kayla didn't care. "So what does this do to the rest of the mystery?" she asked as the others walked away. "What about the cafeteria and everything?"

I frowned. "Well, I doubt if a pack rat is riding one of the horses to the cafe and knocking over the trash cans. So, something else is going on. We'll have to . . ."

"I know," she said in a tired voice, "keep our eyes open."

That night after campfire, we settled in—after we carefully packed all our shiny things away. Dave had an announcement.

"I have some good news and some bad news," he said. "The good news is—you don't have to go to flag-raising tomorrow."

"Yaay!" we shouted.

"The bad news is—you don't have to because you'll already be up."

"Booo!"

"The good news is—we leave on our overnight hike to Thunder Mountain Treehouse Camp at sunrise."

"Yaay!"

"The bad news is—we have to eat sack breakfasts."

"Booo!"

Dave was having fun with it. "The good news is—Bob is carrying most of our stuff there with the horses."

"Yaay!"

"The bad news is—the Mohawks are going with us."

Silence. Not even a boo.

"Come on, guys. Their counselor hurt his knee water skiing. Mrs. Carter has assigned two of them to each of the other cabins. Cody and Alan will be with us the rest of the week."

Peter spoke up. "Isn't the overnight hike supposed to make everyone work together? Isn't it like an obstacle course? Don't we have to help each other just to make it to Treehouse Camp?'

"Yes," Dave replied.

"So how are we going to make it with them?"

"We'll have to try hard to work with them. We can make them feel like part of our team. Remember, we're the ones who claim to be on God's team. Isn't there room for Mohawks there?"

Everyone was quiet again. Then Brian said, "I'll try, Dave."

Luke and I said it at the same time. "Me too."

Peter echoed what we said. Finally, Max agreed. "OK, I'll try," he grunted.

I'm not sure what everyone else thought, but I hoped there wouldn't be any problems. *Whatever happens, I'm sure it won't be all that bad*, I thought as I drifted off to sleep.

Boy, was I wrong.

CHAPTER ELEVEN

The Trail to Treehouse Camp

Day Five

The trail to Treehouse Camp is tough! After a long hike uphill, we came to a narrow pass between two rock cliffs. Across our path was a wooden wall.

"What is that?" Peter asked.

"It's the flattest tree I've ever seen," Luke answered.

Dave laughed. "It's our first obstacle. We have to go over the wall."

"But it's taller than we are," Brian protested.

"That's what makes it an obstacle. You'll have to work together to get over it. And I can't help."

With that, Cody and Alan sighed and dropped their packs to the ground. "Get out of the way,"

Cody said, "I'll get over the wall." He ran at it and jumped as high as he could. His hand didn't reach the top, and he slid down to the ground.

After two more tries, he gave up. As he sat panting, Max said, "Now what do we do?"

I looked at the wall. "If we had some rope, we could . . . it doesn't matter, we don't have any rope."

Cody snorted. "If we brought a ladder, or if we were twice as tall, we could go over it too."

Brian's head popped up. "That's it! Twice as tall! What if we stand on someone's shoulders?"

Cody stood up. "Good idea, Brainy. Alan, come here." He bent down to make a foothold for Alan to step in. "You get up on my shoulders."

Alan stepped up onto Cody's handhold and put one foot on his shoulder. "Whoa! Hold still!" Alan swayed back and forth like he was going to fall.

"I'm trying!" Cody wobbled too.

"Here, hold my arm," I shouted, joining Cody. Alan grabbed my hand and steadied himself. Then he let go and stood up straight.

"Come closer to the wall," he said. Cody did, and Alan reached over and grabbed the top of the wall. He pulled himself up and away from Cody. We backed up to watch him pull up and sit on the top of the wall.

"Hey, after you get here, it's easy!" Alan called. "There's room to sit up here and the other side is like a long slide."

"Great," Max said, "but how do the rest of us get up there?"

"We'll have to do it the same way," I said. Cody looked at me. He was still rubbing his shoulders. "We'll take turns," I said to him.

Brian got up on my shoulders next. He stretched up but couldn't grab the top of the wall. Alan reached down and pulled Brian to the top. "OK," he called down, "that's one."

Cody helped Luke up next. Then I staggered around until Max grabbed the top. It took both Cody and me to get Peter up.

"You next," Cody said when we were the last ones left. I stepped up onto his shoulders and pulled myself up to the top.

"How do we get you up?" Alan asked Cody. Cody shrugged and got ready to run and jump again.

"Wait," I called, "I have an idea." I grabbed the top of the wall and hung down. "Max, you hold my arms. Cody, jump up and grab my belt."

Alan caught on. "I'll reach down and grab Cody and help him up past you. Come on, Cody, do it."

"I hope this works," Max muttered.

"I hope Zack's belt doesn't break," Luke said.

Cody caught my belt on the first try, and Alan had him up in a second. We waited while Dave jumped up and joined us. Then we all slid down the back side.

"Way to go," Dave said. "You guys really worked together."

Cody didn't say anything, but he smiled.

Our next obstacle was a stream. We had to cross it on a vine. "Aaaah!" Luke called like Tarzan as he swung over. The hard part was getting the vine back to the next person. After Max and Cody and I were across, Peter came next.

"Jump!" we shouted, as Peter got to our side. But he didn't let go of the vine. When he swung back out over the water, Max ran to the edge.

"I'll grab him when he comes back," Max shouted. "Somebody grab me."

When Max grabbed Peter's leg, Cody grabbed Max. They were still tilting toward the water, so I grabbed Cody. Finally, Peter let go and we all fell over backward.

I don't know who started it, but the next thing I knew, we were all laughing. Even Cody and Alan.

The rest of the guys got across with no problems. Before long, we came to our last obstacle. "I can see the treehouse," Brian called from in front.

"But we have to cross a bridge."

"What's the big deal? It's just a bridge," Max said as he moved past Brian. Then he stopped. "What's holding it up?"

We all stopped at the edge of the canyon. The treehouse was on the other side. It was only about fifty feet across, but both sides of the canyon wall were very steep. It wasn't too deep, but at the bottom was a fast-running river.

But the problem for us was the bridge. "It's a rope bridge," Dave said. "It's safe to cross, but you have to be careful. If it sways too much, you can tip over the edge and fall. Work together, and you can get across easily."

The bridge was made of ropes tied together. There were wooden slats along the bottom to step on and kind of a web of rope on both sides. A thick rope ran along the top of both sides like a hand-rail. "I don't think I like this," Brian said.

Dave gave us one bit of advice. "It's easiest if one person stands on each end to steady the bridge while the others cross."

"I'll go across first." I stepped out onto the wooden slats of the bridge and grabbed the ropes on both sides. The bridge sank down a little with each step. When I got out near the middle, the whole bridge started to sway from side to side. I stopped and took a deep breath. I looked down at the rushing water, not so far below.

"Keep going. You can make it," a voice called from behind me. It was Cody. He was standing at the end, holding the bridge steadier. I kept going. Before long, I got the hang of walking with the swaying, and it was easy.

"Come on," I called from the other side. "It's easy once you get used to it." With Cody and me on the ends, the others crossed without any trouble. I think Brian crossed with his eyes closed.

I waited while Cody started out. He figured out the swaying faster than I did, and almost ran across. "That was easy," he said as he reached my side. "Let's go across again."

But the others were calling from the treehouse. "Come on, this is great!" So we ran after them.

Treehouse Camp is the best! A rope ladder leads up the side of the enormous tree and into the treehouse. "This place is as big as our cabin," Max said. "And look how far you can see!"

We set up camp, and Dave built a fire in the pit under the tree. "This is the best meal we've had all week," Peter said. "Hand me another hot dog."

When the marshmallows were gone too, we leaned back and watched the stars come out. "We sure are lucky to be here at camp," Brian said.

"This is great."

I agreed. "I can't wait to tell Mom and Dad about this."

Cody snorted. "You guys have it so good. The last time I saw my dad, he punched me in the face."

What do you say after that? I looked at Cody a little differently. Maybe he wasn't just a tough, mean kid. Maybe he felt lonely. And afraid.

Brian felt bad too. "How did you get to come to camp, Cody?"

Cody stared at the fire. "The church people convinced my mom that camp would be good for me. I guess it has been. I mean, I haven't been in any trouble this week. At least, not like I would be at home."

Everyone was quiet for a few minutes, listening to the fire crackle. Then Cody said, "You guys are lucky to believe in God. It must be nice to really believe that someone cares about you and watches over you."

Dave spoke up. "You can believe in God too, Cody. He loves you more than you can imagine."

Cody just stared at the fire. Before long, the others began climbing up to their beds. I was part of the way up the ladder when I heard Cody mumble. "No one has ever loved me."

CHAPTER TWELVE

Lost on Thunder Mountain

Day Six

"We need to get started early today," Dave said the next morning. "There's a chance of thunder-storms this afternoon."

I was first over the bridge again. Dave followed me and sat on the edge of the canyon to watch. Everyone made it across again without trouble, with Cody and me holding the ends steady. Then Cody started across.

"Hey, watch this," he called from the middle of the bridge. He leaned to his left, then back to his right. The bridge started swinging back and forth.

"Cody! Cut that out and come on across," Dave called.

Cody rocked the bridge again, then started on

toward us. "I was just having a little fun," he said. His next step was just a little too far on the right side. The whole bridge tipped.

He grabbed the rope rail and held on for a second. But before I could do anything, Cody fell over the side and splashed into the stream below.

"Cody!" I shouted. I held on tight and leaned as far as I could over the edge of the bridge. Behind me, Dave dropped his backpack and jumped off the canyon wall. Everyone else rushed to the edge and looked down, shouting and screaming.

I watched Dave splash into the water and come up. He looked around for Cody. "Over there," I shouted. "He's down there by that log."

Dave swam down to where Cody was hanging onto a log at the river's edge. Together, they struggled up the bank nearest us.

The guys up on the wall shouted and cheered. I was still watching Dave, and he was trying to tell us something. "Hey, guys! Quiet! Dave's trying to talk."

With everyone quiet, we could hear Dave's voice over the sound of the water. "Zack, we don't have any rope, do we?"

"No," I shouted.

He looked around and said something to Cody. "Is Cody OK?" I asked.

"He hit his foot on a rock, but I don't think it's broken."

Luke shouted, "Dave, how are you going to get out?"

Dave looked at the wall above him and the rushing water. "I don't think we can. You guys are going to have to go back to camp and get help."

Luke looked at me. "Do we even know how to get back?"

I shrugged. "We can go back the way we came. But it took us all day to get here. That's too long for them to wait."

Dave shouted again. "Zack, you guys took tracks-and-trails class, didn't you?"

"Yes."

"There's a shortcut back to the camp from here. It starts at that big pine tree just down the path."

I turned to be sure I could see the tree he was talking about. The big tree was there in plain sight.

"OK," I shouted down at him.

"You should be able to follow the trail markers. If you get mixed up, remember the camp is down-hill. And, Zack, be very careful. Keep everyone together."

I stood up straight and walked over to the guys. "OK, you heard him. Let's go."

Alan took a last look over the ledge, then joined us as we started back down the path. At the big tree, Brian saw the trail first. "This way, Zack. See the marker?"

We started at the spot where a small rock sat on a larger one and followed that path for a long time. We turned when we found rocks that marked a turn to the right or left. Then Brian asked, "Do you think they'll be all right?"

"They're fine," I answered. "Dave said Cody was OK. They'll wait there on the bank until Bob or Mrs. Carter brings the horses and enough rope to pull them out."

It sounded great. Until we came to a place where the trail split. And right where the rock markers should have been was a fallen tree.

"What do we do now?" Max asked. I looked in both directions, but I didn't see anything that would help.

Alan spoke up. "Dave said to keep going downhill. That way seems more downhill to me." He pointed to the right.

"I think he's right," Luke said. It made sense to me, so we turned right. After about twenty minutes, we came out in a meadow, and the trail disappeared. We were completely lost.

"We need to go back to where we were," Peter

said. He sounded really scared.

"Go back where?" Max demanded, pointing behind us. "We have no idea where the path is."

"What can we do?" Peter whined. "We have to do something!"

I stepped in. "What we need to do first is calm down. We can't be too far from camp. We were on the right path for a long time."

We just sat and breathed for a minute. Then Luke said, "Someone should climb a tree and look around. They might see something helpful."

"Good idea!" Everyone liked that. We decided Luke would climb up. Before he did, Brian had another idea.

"I think we should pray," he said. "After all, this isn't just for us. We're trying to help Cody and Dave."

Alan raised his eyebrows. "Do you really think that will make any difference?"

"Alan," I said, "we really believe in God. We really think He cares about us. And about Cody. And you." I didn't know I believed it that much until I said it.

He looked at me for a second. "Then let's pray," he said quietly.

Brian prayed. "God, help us find our way back. You know that Cody and Dave need help. Keep them safe. Amen."

Soon Luke was calling from way up in a tree. "I see a larger clearing in that direction. It might be that farmer's fields you told me about."

We headed that way. I thought we might find a path back from there. I was stepping over a log when Brian shouted, "Stop!"

I froze with my foot in midair. "What is it?"

He pointed to the ground in front of me. "Hoofprints!"

We all bent down to look. "They're big prints," I said. "They must be Tiny's. Which way are the tracks going?"

Everyone scouted around, careful not to cover any tracks. "This way," Alan called out from a sandy spot. "The tracks are going this way." I was headed over toward him when he shouted again.

"Wait a minute—the tracks are going both directions. See?"

Max looked. "He's right. Some of the tracks are going to the left, and some are going to the right. Which way do we go?"

I tried to pay attention to what I was seeing like Cindy taught us in tracks class. Finally, I saw it. "Look! The tracks going to the left cover over the tracks to the right."

"So?" Max asked.

"That means Tiny went that way," I said, pointing to the right. "Then he came back. He must have been heading back to camp. So we go this way—left!"

The guys cheered. I walked in front, slow enough to see the hoofprints. Luke walked beside me. "Why do you think Tiny was out this way?"

"I think I know, but we have other things to worry about now," I answered. "Have you seen how dark the sky is getting?"

Just then, we heard a little thunder behind us. I started walking faster. "That's real trouble," I whispered.

"You mean lightning?" he asked.

"Yes, but worse than that, rain. If it starts to rain, these tracks will wash away. Then how will we find the camp?"

Boom! This time, the mountain shook. "Well, now we know why they call it Thunder Mountain Camp," Luke said.

"Zack," Brian called from the back, "what will happen to Cody and Dave if it rains? Will that river flood?"

Suddenly, everyone was worried. "Not unless it rains very hard," I answered. While I spoke, we heard the first drops hitting the leaves above us.

"Let's hurry," I added.

CHAPTER THIRTEEN

Something Strange and Amazing

Day Six

We hurried as fast as we could follow the tracks. Then, between thunder claps, I heard something. "Wait!" I stopped and held out my hand.

"What? We don't have time to stop. Let's go!"

"Shhh!" I insisted. "Listen."

For a minute, all we could hear was the patter of the rain. Then, in the distance, ahead of us, we heard it.

"Attention, campers. Please stay inside your cabin until the storm is past."

Max jumped straight up. "It's Mrs. Carter on the camp loudspeaker!"

"I never thought I would be so happy to hear that voice," Luke shouted. "Let's go!"

Now we ran, following the sound. We raced right past the horses, past the cafe, and straight to the camp office. We hit the porch, sounding like a stampede. I jumped over a metal chair and slammed into the door. It popped open.

Mrs. Carter jumped back from the microphone. "What is going on here?" Bob jumped up from his chair as if he might have to throw us out.

"It's Dave and Cody," I panted. "They're stuck in the canyon under the rope bridge."

"What?" Bob asked. "Where's your counselor?"

"That's what we're trying to tell you," Max and Peter shouted.

"OK, OK, one at a time," Mrs. Carter said in a loud voice. "You," she said, pointing at me, "explain. Slowly."

"We were leaving Treehouse Camp this morning when Cody fell off the rope bridge. Dave jumped in after him."

Bob interrupted. "Are they OK? Did you see them?"

"They were OK. Dave helped Cody over to the riverbank. He said Cody's leg was hurt but not broken. But they couldn't climb out. The canyon walls are too steep. He told us to come back here and get help."

Five minutes later, Bob and two other counselors rode out through the rain with plenty of rope and a medical kit. We sat in the cafe and told Mrs. Carter everything that happened. Mr. Morgan brought us some hot chocolate.

By suppertime, the whole camp was talking about it. We were telling the story to Ally and Kayla when the horses rode up outside. "It's them!" Brian shouted.

Cody rode behind Bob on Paint. Dave followed on Tiny. "Boy, are we glad to see you," Luke shouted.

They hopped down, and Cody was hardly even limping. We all crowded around. "You're OK," I said to Cody.

"It's just a bruise," he said. "You guys saved us. We were starting to get worried when it took so long. Then when the storm hit . . ."

Alan interrupted. "We got lost. A tree covered the path markers, and we got turned around. But these guys figured out the way home."

"We did it together," I said. "But we were sure worried when the rain started!"

"So were we!" Cody laughed. "Especially when the river started rising. But Bob got there just in time. And Tiny pulled us out with no problems."

It was great to see Cody look so happy. I think he was beginning to believe that some of us really cared about him.

After a few minutes of shouting and cheers, I finally got back to my supper and Ally and Kayla.

I told them how we found the way back. "After we prayed, we found these horse tracks. They were so big, they had to be Tiny's."

"But why would Tiny be going out that way all by himself?" Ally asked.

"Maybe it was a miracle," Kayla suggested.

"Maybe," I agreed, "but I think I know a way to find out for sure. And solve this mystery about the kitchen."

Before I could say any more, Luke ran up. "Zack! Come on, we still have the skit for campfire tonight. We have to practice!"

"See you later," I called back as I ran after Luke.

Our cabin's skit was the crucifixion of Jesus. We had agreed that Dave would be Jesus. He showed us the camp's wooden cross. "It fits into a hole by the campfire bowl. That way, you can make it stand up. And you can hammer these big nails into these holes here." He showed the holes to Cody and Alan, who were to be the Roman soldiers. "It will look real, and it gives me something to hold onto when you stand the cross up."

We practiced for a few minutes, but before long, we were waiting behind the bushes at the campfire bowl. The storm was over, and everyone wanted to sing. Finally, Mrs. Carter said, "Tonight's skit is 'The Crucifixion.'"

First, Peter played Pilate. "This man is not guilty. His blood is on your hands," he said. Then he washed his hands in a big bowl and walked away.

Next, Cody and Alan whipped Dave with grass whips. Dave acted like it was painful. He twisted and turned. When his back was toward the bushes, Luke squirted it with ketchup. "That looks real," Brian whispered.

"Too real," I agreed. It was kind of sickening. When Cody and Alan made Dave start dragging the cross toward the hole, the ketchup dripped and ran down his back. Dave dragged it part of the way, then collapsed into the sand.

Cody grabbed Max, who was standing nearby watching. "You! Carry the cross." So Max carried it the rest of the way, while Cody and Alan dragged Dave.

Brian and I, the disciples, followed them out and stood watching. When they laid Dave on the cross and pulled out those long nails, I thought about what really happened to Jesus. For the first time, maybe, I really thought about what Jesus did for me—to rescue me.

DETECTIVE ZACK

Cody stuck his nail in place and swung the big hammer. Blam! The cross shook, and Dave's arm twitched. Then Alan took a swing at his nail. Blam!

Max stood with us and watched. "We sure picked the right parts for Cody and Alan," he whispered. "They probably think being a Roman soldier is fun. I bet they 'accidentally' hit Dave's finger. Or do something strange."

I kept watching, and sure enough, Cody did something strange. Something no one expected. He stood up and threw the hammer down.

"I won't do it!" he shouted at Dave, with tears running down his face. "If Jesus was a person like you, He didn't deserve to die."

I couldn't believe my eyes. Cody walked over to the edge of the woods and sat with his head down. Alan dropped his hammer and joined him. No one else moved. I think everyone was in shock.

Finally, Dave stood up, dropped the cross in the hole, and walked over to sit next to Cody and Alan. Pastor Mike came up to the front. Everyone was silent when he spoke.

"Cody is right. Jesus didn't deserve to die. But He was willing to die to save us. To rescue us from the sadness of this world. The Bible says that He loved each of you enough to die so that you can live forever with Him.

"Are you willing to follow Him and let Him change your life? He will, and He'll make you a happier person. If you want to follow Him, stand up."

I was already standing up, but I stood straighter. I watched Cody and Alan stand up with Dave as Pastor Mike spoke again.

"You've heard me say that calling yourself a Christian and claiming to believe the Bible don't mean anything if your life isn't different. Remember the Good Samaritan and Zacchaeus?

"If you start following God, you are going to be different—happier, more kind and caring, and more fun to be around."

I looked over at Cody and shook my head. *It is amazing how much God can change a person in just one week*, I thought. *I guess the Bible is right again. Being a Christian really does make you different. If you let God change you.*

Pastor Mike paused and looked out at every face. "Jesus says, in the Bible, that when we're ready to show the world that we're going to follow God, we should do what He did—be baptized. If you're ready to tell the world that you're going to follow God, and let Him change you, then join me up here, and we'll talk about being baptized."

I was the first one there.

Later, on the way back to the cabin, Luke said, "This was the best camp ever. Nothing turned out like I thought it would. But everything turned out great."

"Not everything," I reminded him. "We still haven't solved the mystery at the cafeteria. But we're going to. Tonight. Come on, we have one more trap to set."

Clues About Christians

God did answer our prayer and help us find our way back to camp.

Cody was right. Jesus didn't deserve to die. But He was willing to, so He could rescue me.

I know that the Bible is true. If someone really is following God, that person is different—happier, more caring and kind, and more fun to be around.

I can see how much God has changed Cody in one week. I want Him to change me too.

I want to be baptized and tell the world that I'm really following God.

Thunder Mountain Mystery Clues

Tiny's tracks led us home. But where did he go out there? And who was riding him?

Tonight's trap has to work!

CHAPTER FOURTEEN

Mystery at the Cafe

Day Seven

"Grab your kite string again," I told Luke in the cabin. As we slipped behind the camp office, I snatched two of those cement blocks with holes in them that I remembered from before.

"Grab that chair," I whispered to Luke. He looked puzzled, but picked up the metal chair from the porch. By the time we got to the back door of the cafe, I was huffing and puffing.

The trash cans were lined up along the back wall, as usual. I grabbed the skinny bush that stood next to one end of the row of trash cans. "Help me bend this bush," I said.

"This is no time for bush-wrestling," Luke said. "What are you doing?"

"Look," I explained, "we're going to bend this bush back away from the trash cans. Then we're going to tie it there with your kite string. We'll run the string down through a cement block on this side of the doorway and then across to a block on the other side."

Luke got the picture. "So when someone walks through the back door, they'll trip over the string. It'll break, the bush will pop back up, and crash!"

I nodded with a big smile. "It'll sound like Thunder Mountain Camp, all right. Everyone will hear it."

We got the blocks in place; then I leaned on the bush while Luke tied the string. "OK," he said when it was all tied. I stepped slowly back, and the bush stayed bent. Perfect!

"By the way," Luke said, "what was the chair for?" But by then, I was carrying it around to the side. When I got back, he was busy hiding from two kids with a flashlight.

"Let's go before we get caught down here," he hissed.

The counselors let everyone stay up a little later, since it was the last night of camp. "Keep your flashlight handy," I told Luke. We had barely settled down when it happened.

Crash! Boom! Bang!

Everyone ran to the windows. "What was that?"

"Not another storm, I hope!"

"Is someone out there?"

By the time they stopped asking questions, Luke and I were out the door. As we ran from the cabin, I whispered to Luke, "Turn on your flashlight."

"Why?" he whispered back. "They might see us coming." Suddenly, all the lights in camp went out. Quickly, his light clicked on.

"That's why," I said. "Now, this way."

He wanted to run to the cafe. "They'll get away," he hissed.

"Not if we hurry." We rushed past the office to the little electricity building. Its door was open, so I shoved it closed, then reached for the metal chair I had leaned against the wall earlier. I wedged the chair under the door handle.

"Now what?" Luke asked.

"We wait," I said.

"Wait! What about the thief?" As he spoke, the door knob clicked back and forth. "Hey," he whispered, "someone's in there."

"I know."

Before we could talk anymore, Mrs. Carter came rushing around the corner. Her flashlight lit us up. "Zack! Luke! I'm surprised at you two. I didn't expect to find you out here turning off the lights."

"We didn't," I started to say. But then Bob dashed around the other corner. "What's going on?" he started to say. Then he heard a familiar whinny from the cafe. His flashlight found something very large. "What's Tiny doing out? You two have a lot of questions to answer."

"I think you should ask him," I said, pointing to the door. They watched while I moved the chair and opened it. "Come on out," I called into the darkness.

"I might as well turn the lights back on first," a voice said. With a click, the camp was lit up again. Then Mr. Morgan stepped out.

"Mr. Morgan! What is going on here?" Mrs. Carter was astonished.

"Well, I'm not sure I can say, ma'am," he answered.

"What do you mean?" Bob demanded. "You know something! And you can start by explaining why that horse is here."

Mrs. Carter gasped. "Are you stealing from the cafeteria?"

Mr. Morgan laughed softly. "I didn't say I don't know. I said I can't say. I promised I wouldn't. But no, I'm not stealing. You'll find nothing missing from the kitchen."

Before it got any worse, I spoke up. "Maybe I

can help. Mr. Morgan is using Tiny to carry left-over food to those homeless people at the farm next door."

Now it was Mr. Morgan's turn to look astonished. "How did you know that?"

I explained. "When someone knocked over the trash cans the first night of camp, and then the lights went out, I figured something was going on. Then Ally told me that you put the food that was cooked but not served in a special trash can. And put it in the refrigerator."

He sighed and nodded. I went on.

"I didn't put it together then, though. But Luke and I used that rake, Mrs. Carter, to smooth out the sand behind the kitchen so we could watch for footprints. We were surprised to find horse prints."

Bob shook his head. "I knew someone was messing with the horses."

"Then, I thought I saw one of Tiny's hoofprints in the mud at the stream by the farm. I wasn't sure. But when we were lost in the woods, we found a set of huge hoofprints going one direction and then back. I knew they must be Tiny's, and I hoped someone was using him to go away from the camp and return. It turned out I was right, because we followed them back to camp."

Suddenly, Mrs. Carter thought it through. "Zack,

how did you know Mr. Morgan would be here?"

I shrugged. "I thought he would want the left-overs from today. Luke and I set up a trap that would knock over the trash cans. I figured with all that noise, he'd do the same thing he did the first night—turn the lights off to keep you guys busy while he got away with Tiny. So I put this chair here where I could trap him. Then, all we had to do was get here before he got away."

Mrs. Carter didn't seem so mad now. She laughed a little. "Mr. Morgan, is all this true?"

Mr. Morgan sighed. "It's true. I promised I wouldn't tell anyone that I was bringing them food, but they need it so badly. Especially the babies. Still, I didn't take anything that wasn't going to be thrown away. I just hated to see it wasted when people were hungry."

I patted his arm. "I knew you weren't as mean as you pretended to be. Especially when you made us hot chocolate this afternoon."

He smiled at me.

"I'm sure we can work out something so you don't have to sneak food out at night," Bob said. "Boys, why don't you run back to your cabin now. And thanks for helping us clear this up."

We didn't tell anyone at the cabin about it. If Mr. Morgan needed it to be a secret, then it would be one. But we did have to tell Kayla and Ally the next morning at breakfast.

"That's why he put those trash cans in the fridge," Ally said. "He needed to keep the food fresh until he could take it to those people. I guess he really is a nice man."

Kayla shook her head. "Mom and Dad will never believe all the things that happened this week. Not even from you, Zack."

When I said goodbye to Ally, she said, "I'll see you here next summer, I hope!"

I kind of hope so too.

Luke said he would write. He doesn't live too far from me, so I might see him sometime.

When I told Cody goodbye, he grabbed my hand. "Thanks for being a friend, Zack." I hope he gets to find out more about following God. Knowing Pastor Mike, he will.

I think I learned a lot this week. People who really believe in the Bible, people who really follow God, are different. Even if they don't seem to be at first. Like Mr. Morgan.

I can tell Bobby that real Christians are different. And now I can tell him that I'm going to be a real Christian too. I feel pretty happy about that.

I guess it's true. Following God does make you happier. And it's a whole lot of fun!